INTO WHI

INTO WHITE

WITHDRAWN

RANDI PINK

FEIWEL AND FRIENDS

NEW YORK

A Feiwel and Friends Book
An Imprint of Macmillan

Into White. Copyright © 2016 by Randi Pink. All rights reserved.
Printed in the United States of America by R. R. Donnelley & Sons Company,
Harrisonburg, Virginia. For information, address Feiwel and Friends,
175 Fifth Avenue, New York, N.Y. 10010.

Our books may be purchased in bulk for promotional, educational, or business
use. Please contact your local bookseller or the Macmillan Corporate and
Premium Sales Department at (800) 221-7945 ext. 5442 or by e-mail at
MacmillanSpecialMarkets@macmillan.com.

Library of Congress Control Number: 2016937797

ISBN 978-1-250-07021-0 (hardcover) / ISBN 978-1-250-08690-7 (ebook)

Feiwel and Friends logo designed by Filomena Tuosto

First Edition—2016

1 3 5 7 9 10 8 6 4 2

fiercereads.com

Victor: Let's do this . . .

INTO WHITE

DENT IN HIS JORDANS

On the way to first period, the cheap plastic strap on my book bag broke. The single pink thread that held on for the first six months of school had finally freed itself, dropping hefty textbooks onto Deanté's spanking-new Air Jordan basketball sneakers. With only a handful of black kids at 96 percent–white Edgewood High School, God let my textbooks fall at the feet of the cruelest one.

"Damn, girl! Where you get that broke-down backpack from? Alabama Thrift?" said Deanté, high-fiving two of his friends. "You ain't got nothing to say for yourself? Hey. Your book dented my sneaks. While you picking up those books, buff that damn dent out my sneakers."

I stared at the dent in his red-and-black Jordans. That quarter-sized impression felt bigger than the entire town of Edgewood.

My eyes met Deanté's. There was pity there; I could see it. The same pity that an Asian would have for a fellow Asian, a Mexican would for a Mexican. An Indian for another Indian.

"Get the damn dent out my Jordans!"

I bowed forward to hide the tremble in my chin and the moisture gathering around my eyes. When my knees hit the floor, Deanté's crew doubled over with laughter.

"I knew she would do it, D," someone hollered.

"She's the weakest black girl I've ever seen, bruh," another voice announced.

"Get a backbone, gal!" a passerby yelled on his way to class.

Of all the races in the world, why did God put me in the only one that didn't stick up for one another? No, worse, the one that fights members of its own army: dark-skinned against light-skinned, uppity against inner city, good hair against bad hair; Deanté against Toya. I hated him—more than the insults and the ridicule. I hated that he dropped his *g*'s and added extra syllables to words that didn't deserve them. I hated his dark skin and bad hair. I hated everything about him that reminded me of myself. Deanté and I got the crap end of the stick in Montgomery, Alabama, where black was a disease.

"All right! The dent's been gone, you can get off your knees," Deanté said. But I didn't dare move.

Four sets of Jordans surrounded me—purple and white, red and black, black and gold, and finally, Deanté's red-and-black pair. My knees pressed hard into the linoleum. I wanted the floor to suck me in and take me away from all the Jordans.

"Get up, girl," said the black-and-gold pair.

"I know, right?" scoffed purple and white. "Black girls don't act like that. We need to snatch her black card."

Deanté took a small step toward me and placed his hand on my left collarbone. In my mind, I broke all five of his fingers. In actuality, I did nothing.

"Toya will be just fine when she realizes she ain't white," he said before giving my shoulder a slight squeeze. "Edgewood ain't no place for the weak."

After a string of *amen*s and *ain't-that-the-truth*s, his friends eased to their classes. "Later, D," they said in succession.

After they left, Deanté slid his palm into the crook of my elbow, lifted me to my feet, and rushed in the direction of his friends. "'Ey!" he yelled. "Y'all wait up."

In the distance, I heard my big brother, Alex. "Toya! My God, what's going on?"

"I—I . . ." was all I could get out before my knees buckled. Like always, he caught me before I hit the ground.

And that was it.

That dent in those damn Jordans changed the course of my life.

Later that night, I did something desperate.

"Hey, Jesus?" I whispered, looking out of my bedroom window. "I can't take this anymore. This filth. This curse. This . . . race." I grabbed a handful of skin at my forearm, then my thigh, followed by my breast. Tears fell from my eyes, and I curled into a tight ball at the foot of my twin bed. "I've done everything that you ever asked of me. I've obeyed you. Respected you. Loved you. So, if you ever loved me, please." A giant brown spider crawled along the outside of my windowsill and began spinning the most intricate web I'd ever seen. The next part came out as a whimper. "You said that if I seek you first, the rest shall be added to me. Well, my *rest* is the power to wake up any race I want. Please, Lord, anything but black."

PRAISE JESUS!

I woke up that morning as white as a Bing Crosby Christmas.

Ask and ye shall receive. Seek and ye shall find. Faith of a mustard seed. Seek ye first the Kingdom of Heaven and God can and will turn you white if you're a faithful enough Christian. Christians grew like weeds in Montgomery, Alabama; but awesome Christians, like me, were few and far between.

I squeezed a glob of Palmer's Cocoa Butter Lotion in both palms and polished my knees and elbows out of habit. "No more ashy black elbows and knees. Thank you, Jesus!" I shoved the jug of lotion into the Piggly Wiggly paper bag that I'd recycled into my bathroom trash can.

The thin-toothed comb glided easily through my Barbie blond hair. "Hallelujah," I said to my brand-new doe-eyed reflection.

My nose tooted up to a point. I'd always wondered how white people dug in their noses. With the nostril openings so small, how could they get a full index finger inside? I went for it. It fit fine! From the looks of it, the nostril stretched to accommodate the finger. Awesome. Even their nostrils were cooler than black people's.

"God is so good." I traced a baby-pink line around my thin lips and took a prissy half spin to admire the flattest butt anybody's ever seen. "Praise Jesus!" I hollered.

"Praise Jesus!" echoed my mom from her downstairs bedroom.

"Praise Jesus!" yelled Dad from the other downstairs bedroom.

"Praise Jesus," yawned Alex from the bedroom next door. Praising the Lord was like Marco Polo in my house.

"What are we praising the good Lord for this morning?" my father shouted.

"Does it matter, you old fool?" interrupted my mother. "We're praising God for the sake of praising God! Ain't that right, Toya?"

"Would y'all quit with the fighting?" murmured Alex. The only things my mother and father ever had in common were their mutual regard for *Unsolved Mysteries* and Jesus Christ. Outside of those two interests, they fought about everything.

I blinked at my reflection, and fish-tail braided red ribbon into my celestial hair. "Seriously, thank you, Jesus."

Before my fabulous transformation, I was the color of either a brown Crayola crayon or a cup of coffee with a single hit of cream. I had searched high and low for me-matching shades, and those were the closest. Fingernail-short, tight, dry curls lined my scalp like tiny black pearls. My evil aunt Evilyn called them "cuckabugs," or a head full of naps. Freshman year in high school, she said I looked like a man. Her exact words were *"Girl! You look like a man!"* The following day, I picked a rose and stuck it in my cuckabugs in the hopes of looking more like a girl. I was super satisfied with myself, too, until the ants marched into my ear, down my neck and push-up bra. The whole class jumped when I screamed like a hyena and ran down the hall: another notch in my high-school-loser belt.

"Toya! Come on, you're making us late up there in your precious room!" Mom screamed the same line every morning, but that day her tone was especially harsh. No more procrastination. I quit my primping and cracked my bedroom door. Mom, Dad, and Alex were downstairs waiting.

They stood at the base of the staircase, in front of double anterior doors covered in extravagant tempered glass. The curving banister, oak hardwood, and *Gone with the Wind* chandelier belonged in *Southern Living* magazine. It was an opulence that most Montgomery black families couldn't afford—most including us. Dad slaved daily double overtime and still needed Mom's help to scrape by.

Mom and Dad worked at the Police Dispatch Center, which

received the majority of Montgomery's 9-1-1 calls. Their cubicles were sandwiched together, side by side, and they were in constant competition at work. Who had the highest CPH—calls per hour? Whose calls were most challenging? Who'd received the most caller compliments? They made decent money, but the majority of every penny was reserved for the empty castle.

"Man, do you know that your shirt is as wrinkled as a Pensacola white lady?" Mom spat at Dad.

Dad clenched his teeth and took an extra-large gulp from his black coffee. "Well, if it bothers you so much, why don't you go live with your sister Evilyn, you ole quack!"

A few months back, my mom got fed up with Dad's ridiculousness—his moping, his scruffy appearance, his constant careless coffee spilling, and most of all, his empty castle—and went to live with her best friend and older sister, my evil aunt Evilyn. Mom packed a single duffel bag and ran away from home for a month. I never got a straight answer as to what set my mother off, but I woke up one random Wednesday morning and she was gone.

"That's a new one—*quack*," inserted Alex. "Good word, Dad."

"Thanks." Dad blushed, and Mom poked Alex's rib.

"Ow!"

"I wouldn't have had to come back if you didn't need help paying for your empty castle," answered Mom. "Besides, I couldn't leave my babies to fend for themselves with your crazy tail."

She was right; Dad was at least a little bit crazy. He'd packed up our perfectly comfortable three-bedroom home in the hood for a six-bedroom McMansion near the white people, only he didn't have enough money left over to furnish the thing. You would swear we were rich if you never set foot past the grand foyer to see the five-dollar pillows where the couch was supposed to be. Not to mention the pot of dried black-eyed peas, cornbread, and mustard in the refrigerator where the food was supposed to be. Lord knows, if I had to eat one more black-eyed pea I was going to slap somebody.

To Dad's credit, we could likely afford more food variety, but last year, Mom lost *Taste of Home* magazine's black-eyed pea recipe contest, and she'd become obsessed with perfecting it. She used us as her built-in test kitchen. I liked black-eyed peas, but after a few dozen days in a row, they became nauseating. Mostly, Alex and I fended for ourselves in the food department. Hallelujah for the McDonald's dollar menu.

"Toya, I see your door is cracked up there. I know you hear me!" yelled Mom. "I can't be late again, girl. Your daddy's car keeps breaking down on the way to work and making me late. Come on!"

"She's exaggerating, honey," Dad bellowed, attempting to save face. "My car is just fine. Your mother insists on filling her up with regular gas instead of supreme. The Fiat is a classic! Classics deserve nothing less than supreme."

"Man, you crazy! Who in this house has an extra dollar a gallon to pay for your piece of junk to drink gourmet gasoline?"

I honest to God love my parents, but I'd rather die a double-dead, horrible death than turn out anything like them. I've had a bone to pick with those two since I spoke my first word: *Toya*. How was I supposed to pass for anything but black with a name like Latoya? I asked my mom once if I could change it. I got the paperwork and everything. She told me the name meant the "victorious one" and said no, but when I Googled Latoya, I didn't find any victoriousness, only black women looking like *Damn, why did they have to name me Latoya?*

"Lord have mercy, Toya! Don't make me come up there!" Mom yelled.

It was time. Time to expose Jesus's blessings and reveal myself. My breathing quickened, and sweaty thighs stuck together at the thought of showing my new white self to my old black family. Peeking through my bedroom door, I saw them all congregated at the bottom of the stairs. Dad spilled coffee and didn't even bother to clean it up. Mom's thumbs fixated on a stubborn blackhead on Alex's bottom lip. "Mom! Stop!" He scrunched his face up, but he loved it. My clueless group of misfits was about to see God's greatest miracle since Lazarus; maybe better. This was my moment, and I went for it.

PRESENTING: ME, BUT WHITE

They studied me like a Sudoku puzzle. No one spoke.

Mom broke the silence. "You're such a beautiful girl; I don't know why you wear those ridiculous ribbons on your head. Some girls don't need all of that extra."

"You look pretty, darling." Dad spilled another tablespoon of coffee and swore loudly.

Mom opened her mouth to scold Dad, but Alex interrupted. "We'll knock 'em dead, little sister! You and me, we're gonna be popular. Starting today. Did you do your History homework?" My big brother's biggest desire was to be popular. Second biggest was to make me as smart as him—an uphill battle if there ever was one.

I ran back to the bathroom mirror.

"Where are you going?" Mom shouted after me.

I looked white to me. Was I losing my mind? No, those tendencies didn't develop until your early twenties; I was still a teenager. They came on earlier if you smoked weed, and I wasn't awesome enough to be offered weed, so I had a full four years before the voices started. In a panic, I ran back to the top of the stairs.

"Do I look different to any of you?" I stroked my delicate blond braid with the tips of my fingers.

Dad took a swig of his coffee and choked on the grounds. So gross. "More beautiful every day, my Toya," he coughed.

"Are you feeling okay? You and Alex can take another day if you need to. There's plenty black-eyeds in the fridge." Mom smiled. She had no problem keeping us home for "sick" days. I was usually more than happy to comply.

"Mom, no! We've missed so much school so far, and we still have two months to go. We're going to get kicked out if we keep that up, especially Toya." Alex jerked away from Mom's thumbs.

"Don't exaggerate, Alex!" Mom retorted. "I don't trust that attendance lady of yours. Montgomery white folks older than sixty-five just don't do right. Too much interaction with bigots ain't good for a young person's self-esteem. That's the reason I wish I could homeschool you two in the first place. " Mom glared at Dad.

When he caught her stink-eye, coffee shot through his nose.

"What?" he asked, plugging his nostril with his knuckle. "You know we can't afford for you to stay home."

As a child, our mother experienced unimaginable racism in the Montgomery education system. Mom was the only black kid in her graduating class, and she was terrorized for it—locker vandalized on a weekly basis, gym clothes frequently stolen, and enough racial slurs to last a lifetime. As a result, she'd dreamed of homeschooling Alex and me since KinderCare. The year before we moved to the empty castle, she typed up a full curriculum and everything. I can't remember most of it, but I do recall her plans to teach from the Bible twice daily. Homeschooling would have been her way of shielding us from Montgomery's notorious prejudice. The empty castle squashed her dreams, and I think that was the real reason she hated it.

"It's not the attendance lady. I've been counting myself, Mom," answered Alex. "And can we please eat something other than black-eyed peas for a change?"

"Absolutely not!" she said, giddy with excitement. "The grand prize is three thousand dollars and a family trip to the Cayman Islands. We eat the black-eyeds until the recipe is perfect."

Dad took another swig of his coffee and looked away.

I began the slow, sad walk down the steps, made my way out the door, and realized that I'd forgotten my book bag. "Warm up the car, I'll be right there. And Alex, you dropped something."

"Oh!" He swooped up a partially opened letter lying by his left Converse tennis shoe. "Thanks, sis."

I marched my heavy feet upstairs. The door creaked open, and there was Jesus standing in the middle of my bedroom. I'm not sure how, but I knew it was him.

"Hey," he said.

"Hey," I replied. He was much more personable than you'd think for the Son of God. He reminded me of a cool English teacher.

"Your family cannot see."

"Oh, great idea. That way they can't disown me or make me move out. I get it. You are so smart, Jesus!" I gave him a Jesus-worthy hug, but when I pulled back to look him over, he wasn't smiling. A single bead of sweat crept down his temple. "What's wrong?"

"I've always been quite fond of you, Toya. Have a seat."

"My mom is going to get me if I make her late again," I told him.

He laughed. "Let me worry about your mother."

A few seconds passed before either of us spoke again. I wasn't nervous or anxious like I am when I meet new people, but I wasn't geeking out like the Woman at the Well, either. Was I blowing my opportunity?

"Jesus, am I blowing my opportunity right now?" I asked.

14

He shifted toward me. "You could never do that."

"Do you do this a lot? You know, hang out with people in their rooms? Turn people white when they ask?"

"No."

There was another long pause. He looked to be in deep thought, so I remained silent.

"Toya, listen to me. We chose you for a reason. You are a very special girl." His brow furrowed. "To be honest, my father does not believe that I should be here right now. Nonetheless, I have walked this earth as a human. I understand ridicule. Pain." Another bead of sweat crept down his temple, and he looked so deep into my eyes that I had to look away.

"Look at me," he said.

I lifted my hand to shield my eyes. "Your eyes are too bright."

He let out a little laugh. "Yeah, I can't always control that." He grabbed a pair of Dollar Tree sunglasses from my nightstand. "Here."

"Much better, thanks." His eyes were pewter gray like a sheet of freshly waxed metal. More than his face, his skin, his clothes, his hair, those eyes branded themselves into my memory.

"You're welcome. Now listen: With the exception of your immediate family, everyone will see in you what you wish for them to see. If you need me, feel free to call me. If things get tricky, don't hesitate to ask. We are giving you the opportunity to be whoever you would like to be. But please." Tiny veins reddened the blindingly white whites of his eyes, and a hefty tear fell to the carpet. "Don't lose yourself."

"Okay," I said.

"I love you, baby girl."

And he was gone.

A BRAND-NEW TOYA

"You look better. I was beginning to think you were depressed," Mom said. "Thank God."

Thank God was right. I'd been washed clean of that dirty skin and bad hair. From that moment on, I was going to rule that school. It was the first day of the rest of my life, a brand-new Toya. Oh yeah, I probably needed to think of another name.

We packed into Dad's 1967 Fiat. Along with the empty castle, that car was Dad's way of proving his worth to the white people. It was a cherry-red convertible, dazzling new on the outside and a broke-down piece of crap under the hood. He'd bought it from a jackleg car salesman for way more than it was worth. When he turned the ignition, the air-conditioner vents kicked four puffs of black smoke into our faces.

"I put up an air freshener for you, Toya." Dad flicked the green pine tree dangling from the crooked rearview.

"Lord have mercy. You old fool. Now it smells like pine-flavored gasoline, this piece of junk," Mom hissed.

"Don't call me no fool, woman!" Dad's insults were never nearly as innovative as Mom's.

"Thanks, Dad," I replied, and he flashed a half smile.

After the twelve-minute drive to school, we smelled like sizzling electrical wires and fuel, as usual. Deanté called Alex and me the Edgewood High Mechanics. "Y'all been working at the shop this morning? You smell like you been greasing engines." Deanté's crew would convulse with laughter, slapping backs and stomping their feet. The whole school would stop to investigate their ruckus. How could such a small group make such an uproar? That's how I felt about the black race as a whole, really. Hovering at around twentyish percent of the population, they made such a large presence of themselves. It was so embarrassing.

Edgewood white people, on the other hand, valued perfection in all areas. Running around the block to shed extra fat and reading books to learn extra things. I knew Edgewood perfection all too well, since Monday through Friday I sat behind its generic sixteen-year-old form—blond, and a size two with see-through blue eyes and baby-pink lip gloss. Perfection got invited to prom by the captain of the football team freshman year and wore a corseted purple chiffon masterpiece topped with a tiara. Under the microscope, Perfection's hair was smooth and slim, just like her skin and body and her life. Deanté wouldn't dare make Perfection pinch the dent from his sneakers in the middle of a crowded hallway.

By the time we reached the school sign, my stomach was flipping somersaults, partly from my new whiteness, and partly from Dad's aggressive gear changes. I hated that car with a passion. At the entrance of the school, Dad missed second gear, stalled out, and gave a snaggletoothed grin. Mom had to let her seat up for Alex and me to squeeze through. When I rose, I could feel the eyes staring me down.

The kids at Edgewood vetted every new student from all sides—family fortune, prior academic accolades, and prestige. The last newbie had transferred from an Atlanta academy. A few weeks after his first day, the entire student body knew that he'd been expelled from his previous school for bringing a knife to campus. He was bullied relentlessly, dubbed the Ripper, and ultimately forced into homeschooling. I couldn't even remember his real name. He was, and always would be, the Ripper. That's when I realized I hadn't thought this thing through at all.

Alex elbowed me hard in the ribs. "What are you waiting for? They're all checking us out. I told you this would be the day; I can feel it." Alex bolted ahead. He wore cobalt-blue Converses, faded black jeans, and a green T-shirt that read *Don't Be a Menace, Go to the Dentist.* Any other day, I would've thought he looked great, but that day, a tingle of embarrassment settled in the pit of my stomach.

Right there at the entrance, Mom started hollering at Dad. Alex and I whipped our heads around to find that Mom had a baseball-sized grease stain on the back of her skirt. They started fussing, so I leaped back to the car door. "Bye, Mom. Bye, Dad," I whispered. "You guys can get going now."

They paused their argument. "Bye, guys," they said in unison before clanking off.

Alex darted toward the entrance while I hung back.

The first time Alex and I had walked into the double doors of Edgewood High, our shoulders were pressed together. We felt most comfortable that way. That day I could feel the shiver in his left arm, and I'm sure he could feel the same in my right. But now, all I wanted to do was ditch him and step into God's great purpose for my life. Jesus had visited me. Not as a burnt tree, or a gust of wind, or a bright light at the end of some tunnel. No. He showered his favor upon me, and everybody knows God's favor comes with great responsibility. I mean, Abraham was told to take Isaac to the top of the hill and stab him. All I had to do was give Alex a bit of breathing room.

"Come on, Toya," Alex called to me. But none of them could see me as Toya.

I ran to Alex and whispered in his ear. "I have my period—I have to go to the girls' room."

"Nasty." He shook his head and sauntered into the school. I knew that would get rid of him—for whatever reason, guys were truly disgusted by periods.

"You new?" I didn't even have to turn around. I knew it was Deanté.

"No, Deanté . . . oh . . . uh, excuse me." I felt his eyes beating down on me as I speed-walked to the closest girls' room. I couldn't help wondering how he would treat the white me. Did white people get a pass from Deanté's wrath? Or was he an equal-opportunity a-hole? Either way, in that moment, I wasn't prepared to deal with him.

As I entered the bathroom, other students ran to make their first classes; still, I checked every single stall for feet. My heart punched my chest so loudly it felt like the drum line took a detour through the restroom. Stress sweat made my pits smell oniony and gross, and telltale white-girl pink targets flushed my cheeks, showing the world my awkwardness. I turned toward the mirror to rebraid my hair for comfort. I still couldn't believe the reflection staring back at me. My skin glowed golden, and my eyes sparkled like bright blue marbles. Perfection. Sweaty, oniony perfection, but perfection nonetheless.

"Lord have mercy." I paced back and forth alone in the

bathroom when another dilemma plagued my thoughts. Did I sound white enough? "Lawd, hayuv mercy," I said to my reflection, attempting a white Southern drawl. I threw the back of my hand to my forehead. "Oh, Lawd have mercy." The reflection was right, but the voice was all wrong, and Deanté could spot a phony from a hundred paces. I started to panic. "What have I done?"

I needed to know if I sounded black, so I decided to call the most honest Southerner I knew. I tiptoed out of the girls' room and down the empty hall toward the media center. I let out an involuntary sigh after a quick glance at the magazine display. The April issues of *Teen Vogue*, *Seventeen*, and *Cosmo* were in, hot off the presses. All covers featured the blond, the blue eyed, the skinny, and the white, of course. I stroked my own soft waves for reassurance.

Thank God.

I reached the shiny black no-pay pay phone in the far left corner of the media center. It looked like a pay phone, smelled like a pay phone, felt like a pay phone, but when you picked up the receiver, you got a happy dial tone without depositing any coins. The no-pay pay phone was there for the handful of bused-in students whose parents couldn't afford to give them a cell. Everybody knew that the old-as-dirt, hard-of-hearing media center helper slept on the job, so she wouldn't be a bother. I sat on the counter and dialed my evil aunt, Evilyn. I always felt that my grandmother knew what she was doing when she put *evil* in her name.

"Hello," she said, her voice deeply twanged with sugar-sweet deception.

"Aunt Evilyn? It's Toya."

"Oh, hey there. It's been a while since I heard from you, little girl," she replied. Her nickname for me had always been "little girl," and I'd often wondered if she knew my real name.

"Yes, ma'am. I'm sorry, I've been busy with school and stuff."

"Lies! I know your mama doesn't make you and your brother go to school. Y'all at home every other day. You flunking out? You must be flunking out. Keep that up and y'all are going to be losers. I don't want no losers in my family, you hear? You know your cousin Joyce is in her sophomore year at University of Alabama?"

"Yes, Aunt Evilyn, I've heard." She'd bragged on her daughter's success since as far back as I could remember. In high school, Joyce wore peacoats and pearls year-round to please Evilyn, but she secretly despised her mother. Two days after her graduation, she blazed rubber toward Tuscaloosa, grew a giant Afro, and pawned her pearls for off-campus housing.

"You should model yourself after someone like Joyce. She went a little off the deep end at UA, but she ain't never been no loser. Of course, your daddy's a loser, but he ain't blood. He ain't—"

"All right! Thank you for that, Aunt Evilyn. I have a question for you."

"Yes, baby?" she replied. That voice was like Splenda: You might be fooled at first by the sweetness, but it will leave a damn nasty aftertaste and may just cause testicular cancer in laboratory rats.

"Do I talk white or black?"

"You sound like a white girl to me. Your skin is the darkest in the family, but even when you were a little girl, you always talked proper. You get that skin from your daddy's side, by the way. When you came out of your mama, I knew you would turn black like your daddy, because your ears were darker than the rest of your body. I said, Lord have mercy, that child is gonna be the blackest of all of us, and Lord said it to be true. I was right. You a dark little girl—"

"All right! Thank you, Aunt Evil One, I mean Evilyn." I hung up.

Aunt Evilyn could inhale the joy from a room and breathe out only bad things. I knew it, Dad knew it, Alex knew it, hell, her own daughter knew it. The only somebody in town that didn't was my mother—Evilyn's only real soft spot. Aunt Evilyn treated my mother like a breakable bit of priceless china. Every time Evilyn looked at my mom, her eyes filled up in weird ways like she wanted to cry but couldn't allow anyone to see it. Evilyn was seventeen when Mom was born, and since my grandparents had no business having more children, Evilyn took on my mom as her own. She'd always loved my mother more than anyone or anything on this earth. As a child, my mother all but belonged to her older sister, and in many ways, she still does.

After one last eye roll at the no-pay pay phone, I gathered my things and tipped past the fast-asleep media center attendant and out the door, only to run head-on into Alex.

"What's going on with you?" he asked.

ALEXANDER THE GREAT

My mouth fell open. Alex had radar that beeped like a garbage truck when I was troubled. I was cast as the only black Pick-a-Little Lady in our over-the-top production of *The Music Man*. When the teacher found out that I was failing everything but girls' choir, she kicked me out—*beep beep beep!* My big brother was there. Or that time in ninth grade when I slowly stuttered my way through a passage from *Our Town* in English class, *beep beep beep!* He was in the hallway, waiting to walk me home. I could read, just not in front of all those uppities with their fancy seersucker shorts and Lunchables. Of course my dream in life was to be one of those uppities, but I never claimed to be logical.

As he stared, my palms dampened and dread passed through my belly, resulting in a low stomach growl. For the first time in my life, I was lost for words with my big brother. There he was, brow wrinkled with worry, eyes darting across my face in search of something only he could read.

"You skipped first period," he said, still squinting, searching my face for valid reasoning. I forced my mouth shut, but it was too late. He knew that was one of my facial tics. "That's it, let's blow this Popsicle stand. You got everything?" When I nodded, he grabbed my forearm and pulled me toward the janitor's exit.

"After what Deanté did yesterday, we should've just stayed home, anyway. That bastard. A powerless people turns on itself. That damn Deanté proves it." Alex's breathing quickened.

"Wow, Alex. Did you just come up with that?"

"Nope, Cornel West." He stopped to check around a corner. "Coast is clear. This way," he whispered.

I followed him closely, eager to shift the attention away from me. "We shouldn't skip. You're the one who told Mom we were going to get kicked out if we missed any more days."

"Something's going on with you. I can tell." We tipped down the hall. "You need a day."

"'Ey! 'Ey! Where y'all headed?" My heart jumped at the sound of Deanté's voice.

"My God." I stopped.

"Keep walking, Toya," said Alex, without looking back. "Leave us alone, Deanté!"

"Wait up, dude. We cool, I just wanted to ask y'all something."
I could tell from his voice that he was gaining on us.

"Toya, go." Alex shoved me through the janitor's exit and stayed behind. I pressed my ear to the steel door to listen. "Look, if you don't leave my sister alone, you'll be sorry—I swear it."

"What you gone do?" Deanté chuckled.

"I don't want any trouble." Alex's speech was sharp and strong, which surprised me, since he hated confrontation just as much as I did. "Leave us alone."

"That girl is extra fine. What's up with her?"

"Deanté, stop treating my little sister like Hester Prynne." Something rose from my brother's voice that I'd never heard before. "Don't test me."

I cracked the door to see a mix of fear and confusion in Deanté's eyes. He began backing away. "Aight, then, flunk out if y'all want to."

A few seconds later, Alex slid through the door. "Ready?"

I looked up at him, amazed. "Thanks," I told him, not wanting to address the threat. "Who's Hester Prynne?"

He took the books from my hands and mussed my hair. "Wait, you're serious?" I shrugged and he continued, "*Scarlet Letter?*"

"Never read it," I said.

"Toya!" He threw his hands up. "Hester Prynne is the lady

who has to wear a red *A* because she committed adultery in Puritan Boston in 1642."

"And how am I anything like her?"

"Because the crowd gathers to witness her public humiliation. Toya, I know you're not a Puritan." He laughed at his own joke. "And you're definitely not a floozy. Come on, I have a copy in my room. Let's go home."

Our empty castle was a sturdy three miles away, with the last quarter mile all uphill. No *Sound of Music* rolling hill, either—I'm talking full-on stall-out-a-stick-shift, burn-your-legs-off, heart-attack hill. It was the tallest, most daunting hill in Edgewood—almost impossible to conquer.

When we first moved to Edgewood, I named it "the big hill," but after a few failed climb attempts, Alex rechristened it after his favorite X-Men character, Colossus. In his comic's mutant form, Colossus is by far the strongest member of the team. At almost eight feet tall and made of steel, he towers over Wolverine, Cyclops, and of course, Professor Xavier. Alex loves Colossus because he could easily use his height to intimidate or strong-arm, though he never does. Instead he's soft-spoken, honest, and sweet-natured. Alex once told me he thought Colossus would make the perfect Alabamian. Only he was from *the Alabama of the future*. Alex said the phrase in passing, but it stuck with me since I knew what he meant.

The Alabama of the future: where Deanté's reign of terror is finally finished. *The Alabama of the future:* where Alex's kid sister doesn't ask God for the power to change her race.

Colossus, the big hill, was an hour away from Edgewood High on foot, an hour and a half if we stopped at Brookland Mall to go fishing for quarters in the fountain. Which meant I had at least a sixty-minute walk to convince my black sibling, birthed of our black mother, fathered by our black father, that I was white.

By the time we'd cleared school grounds and entered the creepy foot trail in the woods, the naked tree limbs cast eerie shadows that made the path floor look alive. I usually quick-walked through, but that day I took my time. "I got something going on that I need to tell you about," I said, already chewing at loose skin on my fingernail bed.

"I know you're really a sophomore," he blurted.

"What?" Alex always attempted to guess the topic rather than exercise patience and listen. He was rarely correct. No, scratch that—he was never correct.

"I know that you don't have enough credits to technically qualify as a junior, but I'll fix that. I asked Mrs. Roseland if you could do some extra credit to make up those missed tests. She agreed. I'll ask a few of your other teachers later this week. I wanted word to get around in the teachers' lounge that your big brother cared enough to ask. Teachers like that type of stuff."

"What do you mean I'm really a sophomore?" I asked. "I'm taking junior-level English."

"I blame Mom and Dad. I read a study about tiger moms; they're, like, the ultimate helicopter parents. They destroy their kids' toys if they don't do their homework. Destroy! Like bite the head off the Barbie, and stab Cabbage Patch type stuff. That's why their kids wind up at Harvard and Yale and places. The only thing our parents ever made us do was watch reruns of *Unsolved Mysteries*. Actually, I think they might be certifiably insane." His eyes darted around the woods, and he dropped his voice to a whisper. "Do you think we should have them committed?"

"No, Alex. Where would we go? Foster parents in Montgomery, Alabama, would turn us into Miss Celie and Harpo slaves like in *The Color Purple*." I realized I should probably look into that whole sophomore thing. "I have something to tell you, seriously."

"Found one!" He bent down to snag a dirty quarter. Since our parents never adequately stocked the refrigerator with anything other than freaking black-eyed freaking peas, we had a running quarter collection game. Quarters are everywhere if you look hard enough. Every day we gathered as many quarters as possible and pooled them together for dinnertime McChickens and the occasional Quarter Pounder. Alex always won. He was a quarter-spotting genius. I swear, the thing could be half-buried a mile up the road and he would say, *I think I see a quarter up ahead.*

"I have something to tell you," I repeated. "Did you hear me?"

"Did you hear *me*? I found another quarter," he said, amazed that I wasn't more excited.

At that point I realized there was no ideal time to tell my brother. I decided to rip off the Band-Aid. "I'm white," I blurted.

He twirled the found quarter between his thumb and index finger. "It's a bit bent. Do you think McDonald's will still take it?"

"Alex!" I squealed, getting frustrated. "Listen."

"All right, all right." He glided the quarter into his pocket. "What do you mean you're white? Like white as in white? Or white as in white?" He was dead serious, too.

"White." I unbraided my hair and held it out for him to touch. "Here, feel this. Jesus said that my family wouldn't see me as everybody else does, but maybe you can feel the hair. Try it."

My brother looked at me like I had morphed into a green baby alien. His shock was mixed with fear and pity. Like, *How are we going to take care of this green baby alien? It's so little and helpless and insane.* He said slowly, "Toya, it's going to be okay. I think our home life has given you a special PTSD thing."

"What's PTSD stand for?" I couldn't help but ask.

He held the back of his hand against my forehead. "Post-traumatic stress disorder. I'm pretty sure our parents, in combination with the hyper-extremist Christian South, have given you hallucinations about talking to Jesus. We should get home so we can do some Britannica research."

A few years back, Mom found an almost full set of dingy brown Encyclopedia Britannicas at the Alabama Thrift. It was missing the first couple of volumes, so if we needed to know about arthritis or cancer or Botox, we were SOL. "Oh! I found another one!" He picked up a dirty quarter. "I've got enough for a McChicken *and* a small fry. I'll tell you what, if you table this white issue until we get home, I'll give you three-fourths of the McChicken instead of half."

He really was the best. "Okay," I said. "But can we stop by Brookland Mall on the way home to fish the wish fountain?"

"Sure. Thatta girl." He petted my shoulders. "We should fish the arcade, too. Some of the little kids walk away without getting their return quarters. What kind of idiot would leave twenty-five whole cents behind?" He shook his head and walked on.

Brookland Mall was snob central. Any mall with a Gus Von March gave me the I'm-not-worthy heebie-jeebies. If rich old white ladies could choose where they would die, it would be Gus Von March. When the store opened at ten, they bum-rushed the doors with their fancy walkers and hand-carved canes. The day cream was a hundred dollars for the three-ounce carry-on jar; it must've soothed their hearts, because it sure as hell didn't work on the wrinkles. The designer ballet flats had mice faces on them and cost five hundred dollars. I liked those shoes, but I could draw a mouse face on a pair from the Mission Thrift Store for fourteen quarters.

I didn't want to go to Brookland Mall, but I knew my words would never be enough to convince Alex. I was going to take my brother to the mall and prove to him that I was white.

Across the street from the mall sat a skinny-people grocery store, the kind where you could taste whatever fit in the little clear cup, and where you got peanut butter from churning a giant vat of peanuts. One of our traditions was to stop in and jam the juice, our secret slang for sampling our stomachs full.

"You jamming the juice?" Alex asked.

"No, my stomach's upset," I said, holding on to my grumbling abdomen; it always gave away my nervousness. "I'll wait for you out front." When he disappeared inside, I plopped down in one of the silver patio chairs. The sun beat down especially hard in Gump-town that afternoon. Small beads of sweat dripped from my chin, so I held my head back and closed my eyes to relax.

Jesus help me, I thought. It was a prayer I'd prayed many times before. I'd prayed it as a small child, asking my mother for some worthless toy at the Hobby Shop. I'd prayed it in middle school when the hierarchy began to form, and Alex and I realized we were dead last in the lineup. I'd prayed it sometimes without even realizing it—the rope-climb test in phys ed, the PSATs. But the prayer was different now. Jesus was there and tangible in ways he'd never been before. He was absolutely and unequivocally listening.

"Beautiful day, isn't it?"

I jumped. When I opened my eyes, a college-aged guy with dirty-blond hair, white teeth, and an Abercrombie shirt towered over me.

I scrambled to get myself together, sit up straight, and pat the sweat off. "Oh. Yes. Yes, it is," I said softly.

"Anyone sitting here?" He flashed his teeth again. They bucked slightly big for his face, but they fit in his mouth. I nodded for him to sit. Besides, this presented a perfect opportunity to choose my accent. I figured I should try a twang other than Alabama, because Montgomery folks could spot fake Southern better than Roger Ebert.

I attempted thick Boston white. "Great idear, let's tawwk, shuaa."

He paused. "Whoa! Where are you from? That's the strangest accent I've ever heard." I shrugged and wondered whether I should keep talking or run away. "I'm actually really good at this type of thing." He straightened his back in the way guys do when they're trying to appear capable. "I'm a theater arts major at the private college down the street. It's a really exclusive program. I had to audition, like, six times and then they gave me a slot. Do you watch

Fox News in the mornings?" When I nodded, he eagerly took his seat. "The lead anchor's oldest son is in my fraternity cohort. His name's Marshall and he's a total douche, but we do Fox interviews, like, all the time. Do you recognize me?"

This guy was hitting on me. I'd never been hit on by anyone in my life. Maybe it was his teeth, but I can't say I enjoyed it. It felt like a bit of an invasion of space. He just plopped himself down and started talking about his oh-so-very-important college life when all I wanted to do was have a two-way conversation with the Lord Almighty.

"Minnesota?"

"What?" I replied.

"Is that where you're from?" I shook my head. "Alaska, like Sarah Palin?" I shook my head and realized I should trust Aunt Evilyn and stick with my own speech. "Seattle?" I frowned. "I'm sorry, I have an idea. Hey! I'll just go through all the states, and stop me when I nail it."

Alabama, Alaska, Arizona, Arkansas, California, Colorado, Connecticut . . .

"What's going on here?" Alex snuck up, holding two clear sample cups of broccoli salad.

"Who the hell are you?" Abercrombie guy said, jerking his head from Alex to me, then back again, over and over.

"You know this boy?" he asked, as if associating with Alex was the most disgusting thought ever. I shrugged and averted my eyes.

"She's my sister!" Alex yelled.

The guy stood up and strode toward Alex. "Lower your voice, weirdo."

Alex forced eye contact with me. "Toya, get up, now. We're going."

I gathered my things.

"Wait, you're actually with this kid? You don't look like a Toya," he said, mesmerized. "This is bizarre. I'm out." The guy ran off so quickly that he turned into a dirty-blond blur.

When I finally looked at Alex's face, it wasn't anger; it was more like a disappointed dog watching you stuff the last mouthful of a McRib. That was the look Alex gave me in that moment: pure, unadulterated sadness. "Why didn't you tell him I was your brother?"

I dug my fingernails into my thigh. "I don't . . . I mean. I'm white now. I told you—"

"Let's go fishing in the fountain." He barreled toward Brookland Mall.

"Alex, hey, I'm really . . . whhhh . . . I mean, I'm . . . ," I said, struggling to catch up. I hated myself. Not necessarily for being a backstabbing turncoat of a sister, but because I could never find the appropriate words in difficult situations. Sometimes I tried to fight through the mental block, but the words always came out misshapen and made me feel crazy. Then sometimes I blurted the words, and they felt even crazier. In my mind, my comebacks were clear and concise; in reality they were confusing and frustrating, so more times than not, I chose to keep my mouth shut.

"Found one!" He spotted a quarter in the Gus Von March handicapped zone. He'd elected to stuff the hurt down deep and move forward. Never a good idea for a guy with a photographic memory. He could remember his second, third, and fourth birthdays, and everything since; so I knew he would recall being dissed by his beloved little sister in front of the overpriced health food store. I had to make him see and quick.

"You're totally winning. Hey, can we stop in Gus Von March?" I asked.

"I hate Gus Von March. The cosmetics counter chicks eyeball me like Alabama's Most Wanted, and not to mention the lone dude worker. He eyeballs me for different reasons." He glanced around and whispered, "I think he wants to give it to me."

I laughed. "He doesn't want to give it to you." But really, I thought he did. "Just for a few quick minutes, pleeaaassse."

"You hate Gus Von March just as much as I do. Why do you want to go there so badly?"

"Uh . . . I want to see the mannequins for thrift store ideas," I lied.

"Fine, as long as we're in and out."

We went for the same slice of the revolving door and crashed into each other, spinning a full revolution and a half before falling out into the store. The cosmetics ladies gawked at us like we had no home training, as my mom would say. Meanwhile, I could've sworn the lone dude worker checked out my brother's butt when he was picking up his book bag. Though to give the guy a little credit, three full inches of Alex's butt crack were O-U-T out! He and my dad had no butt crack consciousness at all. One time as an experiment, I sat on my bed and rolled my jeans down three inches in the back. Afterward, I decided that there is no way anyone could expose three inches of their butt crack without feeling a breeze.

As we gathered ourselves and our stuff from the marble-ish floor, the cosmetics ladies and gentleman pretended to look away. But I could still see them peeking through their respective glass cases. One clever middle-aged Lancôme lady held her compact high enough to see our reflection instead of staring dead on; she got an A-plus for effort on that one. Even the piano lady gaped from her piano-lady perch. She didn't miss a single note of her rendition of "Flight of the Bumblebee," though she had long abandoned her sheet music. Must've had the thing memorized, or maybe it was one of those programmed pianos, and she was there for embellishment. Either way, it was fertile breeding ground for trouble in the prejudiced South, and I was about to add a pinch of Miracle-Gro to their hotbed. Hell, I didn't make their minds narrow; I was just cultivating the seed that yearned to break soil for sunlight.

Lancôme lady won for creativity. "Can we stop by the Lancôme counter real quick?" I asked. Alex rolled his eyes and shrugged a disapproving approval. The Lancôme lady put down her compact.

"Excuse me, ma'am, would you match my foundation?"

She pursed her lips. "Fine." She shook a bottle of liquid foundation, unscrewed the top, and wiped a glob on my cheek. "There."

Alex laughed. "Wow, lady, are you color-blind?"

"Actually, boy, I see color just fine. How about you?" She looked like a woman standing over fresh diarrhea.

Alex tugged my arm. "Let's go." He glanced around to see that other people were staring. "Now."

Alex, and every other black man in Alabama, had a sixth sense for discriminatory situations. He knew the exact moment to tuck tail and retreat.

"Wait. I have one more question for the Lancôme lady." I turned toward her. "What *exactly* were you doing with that mirror? It looked a little high for a nose powder."

She did a quick two-step. "I was . . . uhh . . ."

"Yeah, that's what I thought!" I said, voice rising. Alex looked on in astonishment, since I'd never raised my voice in public. Even now I felt perilously uncomfortable, but I needed to prove my race to my brother, which sounded ridiculous even to me. "You surprised to see a girl like me hanging out with a guy like this?" I tilted my head toward Alex.

"Toya, that's really mean." Alex wore the McRib-disappointed-dog gaze again.

Lancôme lady's eyes grew to double size. "Toya? You don't look like a Toya. Is this man making you do this? Security!" she yelled.

"And just what is that supposed to mean? No! He's not making me do this! Why would you even ask such a thing? That's incredibly offensive!"

Alex grabbed my elbow and tugged, as two big security guys jogged toward the counter. "I didn't mean anything by it, I mean . . . Toya?" she chuckled. "You know . . . and he's, well." Her eyes said it all, but not enough to convince Alex, who looked more confused than ever.

"Do you mean because I'm white and he's *black*?" I channeled one of Mom's screams.

"Toya!" Alex replied.

"Well . . . yes," she said gracelessly. Alex tilted his head toward the Lancôme lady. "You know, it's not something you see every day 'round these parts."

I knew I could count on good old Gus Von March.

"What do you mean, *well, yes*?" Alex scrutinized Lancôme lady's face for an answer, then he looked at me.

"I told you, Alex," I said, wiping the liquid foundation from my face. "I'm white."

That moment, the security guards reached us. "Is this man bothering you, ma'am?" Guard number one placed his hand firmly on Alex's right shoulder, and guard number two placed his hand firmly on his left.

"Not at all, Officers." I smiled. "We were just leaving."

Done and done.

A PLAN

My tiff with the Lancôme lady drained every ounce of mental acuity from my brain. For the next four point something miles, I was zombified. Thankfully, Alex grabbed hold of the conversation and never let go.

"Toya, do you know what this means? This means God is back and in full effect. You might be one of his New Age disciples, like, the first black female to have a seat at the table. They'll have to redo the Last Supper! But would you be painted as a white girl or as a black girl? We'll cross that bridge when we get there." He scratched his head like he always did when making sense of the impossible. "How will we get you enrolled in school? Where will we say black Toya has gone off to? Of course, no one would notice, since we're absent so much anyway. We can just say black Toya's dropped out or something." He stopped walking and I slammed into his back. "Toya!" He grabbed my shoulders and hugged me tight. "You're white!" His laugh echoed through Edgewood.

He devised numerous plans of assimilation; he said I could be a barely English-speaking exchange student. "Swedish! Dank-a you vwantta go to da movies after skewl? Swedish is like pig Latin, easy peasy coupled with your towhead. Perfect. What do you think?" He went on without a response. "We should watch Dad's *Trading Places* DVD with Eddie Murphy and Jamie Lee Curtis. She did a pretty good Swedish accent on the train when the guy pretended to be the other guy, you know."

I did know. Her breasts bounced like water balloons in that movie.

"I don't know about Swedish, Alex. You know that I suck at making up stories as I go. I'll stumble all over myself and screw it up. What if I'm just white? Aunt Evilyn says I talk white."

"Evilyn is the devil's spawn." He scowled. "And what does talking white mean anyway?"

We'd had this conversation many times before. *Talking white* means something totally different to Alex. He equates *talking white* with proper English, which he says should never be reserved for only the white community. On the other hand, my idea of *talking white* is an all-encompassing attitude—more of a transformation

44

than simple vocal inflection. Moreover, to succeed at *talking white*, a person must embrace the act of *being* white or it won't work.

A few weeks ago, I attempted it. I consulted what I considered to be the handbooks of white females everywhere: *Cosmo*, *Seventeen*, and *Teen Vogue*. I combed those magazines for tips on how to become as white as a natural-born black girl could possibly be. *Cosmo* and *Seventeen* argued that I should wash my hair at least once a day. "So be it," I said. *Teen Vogue* highly suggested boy shorts underwear instead of granny panties. "So be it," I said. All three magazines agreed brown mascara was more natural than black, so I followed the instructions to a T.

My hair started to break off, which I'd assumed was the transition from thick, unruly curls to long, flowing locks. The boy shorts underpants rode up my butt crack so that they turned into bunched-up thongs. The brown mascara made my black eyelashes look like brown recluse spider legs. My bubble really got busted when I marched past Deanté and the other black people perched by first-period biology. He said, "Why you talking like that? You ain't white."

He was right. I needed to make the thing official, so I went to the one person with the power to grant my wish: Jesus. And wouldn't you know it, he swung by my bedroom and made me white.

Alex nudged me. "You ready for Colossus?"

"Not in the least," I said. But I had no other choice. The first twenty-seven steps took the remainder of my energy. I stopped cold.

"I counted twenty-seven steps." He sounded appalled. "Aren't white people supposed to have more endurance?"

I bent forward, gasping for breath. "I need a break." I sat on the edge of the curb.

"Colossus just kicked your butt. We were getting better, too. Last time, it took us six and a half minutes to conquer." He took a seat on the curb beside me. "Our goal is two steps a second, remember?"

Alex had been assessing our steps versus the time it took to get to the top of the hill. One day, *for the sake of science*, he'd conquered Colossus twelve times by himself, carefully measuring his stride and step count to ultimately determine our goal of two steps per second. We hadn't even been halfway up when I stopped.

"Hey, Alex. Why did you accept my change so quick?"

"I see you struggle, Toya." He retied a loose tennis shoe lace and scratched caked dirt from the sole. "You're strong, but these Edgewood people are like your kryptonite. They kill your spirit every day. I've been praying, too, little sis."

"What were you praying for?"

"Mostly for God to bring your smile back. I knew that he could do it, because he can do anything. The question was how,

you know? I must say, though, I never would have imagined this."
He placed his hand on my hand. "He works in mysterious ways."

I smiled, since he'd officially accepted my crazy story as fact
with very few questions asked. "I love you very much. You know
that?"

"I do. Now, come on, white girl." He leaped to his feet. "Don't
let Colossus get the best of you."

When he stood, the sharp corner of a letter peeked from his
pocket. "What's with the letters?"

He stuffed the letter deep down and out of sight. "It's nothing, really."

"They come almost every day now, and they're on fancy paper.
Seriously, what are they?"

"Toya, drop it." He walked ahead.

He'd been guarding the mailbox since he'd started his senior
year, and I had no idea why. Aside from the gross puberty stuff,
we never held secrets from each other; so not telling me about the
letters hurt. However, in that moment, Colossus hurt worse. Every
leg muscle banded together, chanting in protest, *Stoppp, you dirty
heffa! Waaaait, you filthy mutha!* I pressed on slowly, one foot after the
other, and another after that one, too, until I conquered Colossus.

Gasping for breath, we assumed the position.

"All right, fists in the air and biceps to the sky," he announced
between breaths.

"I know, Alex. Come on."

"No need to get snappy. Just because you're white doesn't mean you get to—"

"Come on!"

"Fine. One . . . two . . . three!"

"Colossus the great,

Colossus the cruel,

Alexander and Latoya brought down your rule.

Colossus, you're tall,

Colossus, you tower,

But you will never conquer the Williams sibling

power! HUUAAAHH!"

When we first moved to Edgewood, neither of us could walk up Colossus without taking breaks. We made up the chant after we finally walked it without stopping.

It was time to head home.

With the empty castle in our sight lines, we saw Hampton Williams's large head bobbling its way up the driveway. Half pit bull, half chow chow, and full-blooded demon toward anyone other than the four of us. He had broken loose from his restraints again. Luckily, the Alabama Power Company hadn't picked today to shut off the power. A few months back, when our bill first went red,

Dad came up with the genius plan to tie Hampton on the side of the house where the power box was located. No power man would dare attempt to get past such an animal. Once, a shaky cable guy banged on the door, yelling, "Mr. Williams! We need you to move your dog!" He stood there banging for nearly an hour. The man finally stormed off when Dad blasted Cat Stevens on his ancient surround-sound stereo system.

Hampton, Alex, and I found the house just as we'd left it, bare. Hampton smelled like a garbage dump and left little golden hairs all over the place, but we were so excited to have him inside that we didn't care. He was a loyal friend with a bad attitude like Kanye West. I dragged myself and my dog up to my room, threw myself into bed, and fell asleep before my head hit the pillow. I woke to the clamor of Mom and Dad fumbling with the front door.

"You crazy as hell, woman!" Dad bickered.

"No! You are!" Mom replied. They were like little kids fighting over a Kit Kat.

Hampton sat patiently at my bedroom door, staring at the doorknob as if willing it to open. After rubbing at my eyes, I saw half of a french fry on my side table, and quickly realized someone had hijacked my portion of the McDonald's. When I locked eyes with Hampton, he dropped his gaze to the carpet and let out a pitiful whimper. He'd undoubtedly eaten whatever deliciousness Alex had left for me.

"Toya! Alex! It's time for *Unsolved Mysteries*. We're late getting home because your dad's car broke down on Malfunction Junction again. He made me get out and push on the freeway," she tattled. "I asked the Lord to protect me from oncoming traffic and he did. Praise God!"

"Praise God!" echoed Alex.

"Praise God," I said just loud enough for them to hear.

"Praise God, but it didn't go like that at all, kids! She can't drive a stick, so she had to push. Plus, I made sure there were only a few cars left when I told her to get out," he re-tattled.

"Man, you must be senile," said Mom.

"No, I'm not," he replied. "That's it. I'm going for a walk." I heard the front door open. "Hampton! Come on."

Hampton gave my door a single, respectful scratch, careful not to leave an indent. "That wasn't right what you did—stealing my dinner like that," I said before cracking the door. He took off down the stairs. When he reached the foyer, his unkempt toenails lost traction on the oak floor, and he barreled headfirst into Mom's knees.

"Ouch! Hampton!" she yelled, and he tucked his tail. "Aww," she said before squatting to scratch behind his ears. "I didn't mean to yell at you, buddy."

"Why does the dog deserve an apology, but I don't?" Dad asked sharply.

She stood to meet his line of sight. "The dog didn't move us into this empty house," she said with her hand glued to her hip. "The dog doesn't spill coffee all over the floor. The dog—"

"Come on, Hampton," Dad interrupted.

"What about *Unsolved*—" The front door slammed behind my father before my mother could finish. "*Mysteries?*"

Winston and Camilla Williams, middle-aged tattletales with mutual zeal for *Unsolved Mysteries*. They bickered constantly, but they were hopeless without each other. They were like inoperable Siamese twins, conjoined at the heart. This became glaringly apparent when Mom went to live with Aunt Evilyn.

The threats were nothing new. Over the years, when Mom got mad or irritated at Dad, she'd say, "Don't play with me, man. Or I'm going to live with Evilyn." I'd heard it so often, it started to blend in as a part of our household, like black-eyed peas and praising the Lord. Then one day, it wasn't a threat. Mom actually left.

There was no one event that tipped the scale; nothing earth-shattering. After what was just another day of running late for school and work, and breaking down in the Fiat—a typical Williams Tuesday morning—Mom had enough. By Wednesday she was in the wind.

Since he sat next to her all day at work, Dad took it the hardest. He went through three distinct phases: internalized anger, deep depression, and finally, complete and utter confusion. The first two were mildly tolerable. Internalized anger consisted mainly of midnight walks with Hampton that sometimes lasted until dawn. When he walked, he looked like a man in prayer. Sure, he loved Jesus as much as any Southern-born man, but walking was his true religion, where he found peace in his scattered brain. The soles of his cheap white tennis shoes could be worn to the concrete, and he'd still walk the dog all night long.

Tack a six-pack of Bud Light onto the end of the first phase, and you've got phase two, deep depression. The little free time he had between bleak 9-1-1 calls at work and aimless walks, he'd slump on the couch, drinking and watching reruns of *Unsolved Mysteries* alone. Every now and then, Dad would say, "Camille would've loved this episode." And once, he said, "Kids, I love your mom more than life." I never knew if he was being honest about his feelings for the first time, or drunk.

Dad stayed in the complete-and-utter-confusion phase for the whole month. It was a horrible time. I worried about him from the moment I woke up in the morning until I fell asleep at night. All I knew to do was pray, and I did so faithfully. I called on the Lord from my upstairs bedroom every single day of that month, invoking every ounce of God's grace to help my father hold his head up again, reciting the Lord's Prayer and singing hymns with my fingers clasped together so tightly my knuckles hurt.

It broke my heart to watch my mild-mannered father morph into a mush of a man, constantly rummaging through drawers and closets, looking for God knows what. He once spent an entire Saturday searching for a can opener. When night fell, he began stabbing a can of Glory greens with a paring knife. He almost cut his finger off, of course, and the three of us spent the night in the St. Andrew's Hospital ER. In the waiting room, Dad bled clean through four thickly wrapped gauze bandages. When the doctor finally called us back, he glared at my father with unmasked judgment and said, "Night drinkers bleed like stuck pigs."

When the doctor left the room, we tipped out of the hospital without discharge papers and stopped by the drugstore for a monster pack of big daddy Band-Aids. I haven't seen my father drink a drop of alcohol since that night.

Praise God!

Mom's absence was all around us. In the empty bathroom counter, where the brush filled with her brownish shed-hairs usually sat. In the fuzzy gunk in the dryer's lint catcher, which overflowed and nearly caught fire. The only glimmer of joy was the stack of frozen pizzas that replaced the black-eyed peas. She'd left Alex and me alone with our domestically clueless father. In the end, it was up to us to locate the hidden can opener, which turned out to be in the laundry room (washing powder was in the kitchen, FYI).

Mom opened the front door and yelled after Dad. "Our show's on! It's the one about tumor-sniffing dogs!"

Dad hadn't gotten far, because a few seconds later, he burst through the front door to take his rightful place on the living room pillows next to Mom.

Alex and I collided at the top of the stairs. "Here's this." He handed me a well-read copy of *The Scarlet Letter* before heading down the stairs.

"Thanks, I'll go put it in my room," I said, watching him shuffle down the stairs.

Alex had changed into his blue-and-green-plaid pajamas. He wore a bright yellow tube sock on one foot and a black ankle sock on the other. When he reached the bottom of the stairs, he slid on the hardwood and nearly fell. I never understood why more girls weren't attracted to my big brother. He was the smartest, sweetest, most fascinating guy in Edgewood, maybe the entire state of Alabama.

I went back into my bedroom, and again, there was Jesus.

"You good?" he asked.

"I think so."

He held his hand open and beckoned for the book. After I placed it in his palm, he thumbed through it once and said, "May I?"

When I nodded, he and the book vanished.

We gathered on the living room pillows, lit the fireplace with newspaper (for ambience, not heat), and watched *Unsolved Mysteries* as a family. Mom slid close to me and attempted to squeeze an already popped pimple on my cheek.

"Mom, seriously, quit it," I said, scooting out of her reach.

She frowned and folded her arms, defeated.

"That's mean, Toya," Alex whispered.

"Sorry, Mom. It's just, squeezing makes it turn a little red."

Alex laughed, and I elbowed him hard in the ribs. "Ow!"

"Hush, kids. This is the best part," Dad interjected.

As Mom predicted, that night's episode discussed dogs that could prophesy tumors in their owners. Small potatoes compared to a dog that could keep his family's power on for three months and counting. Afterward, everyone dispersed to their cubbies and settled in for the evening.

On a regular day, seven p.m. meant reruns of crappy television followed by an hour of social media stalking in the upstairs bathroom. Mom bought a dinosaur of a computer from Lenny's Pawnshop at the beginning of school last year. She'd traded a pair of Diamonique earrings and one of her few beloved gold rings for it. It rested on the bathroom counter, since that was the only place in the house where we could steal the neighbors' Wi-Fi, but that night things were different.

I ironed my fanciest ensemble of pink stretchy capris and white lace BCBG top that I'd found stuck between old-lady blouses at the thrift store. My clothes fit so much better as a white girl; no badonkadonk to eat up my panties and no hungry hippo hips to tug at the seams of my capris. Everything in the world was made for white girls. Clothing, magazines, curling irons, makeup, shampoo, and every decent Disney princess. Even Princess Tiana was created and directed by white men; that's probably why she wasn't as awesome as the rest.

I pushed back my cuticles and painted my toes to create the illusion of a pedicure. I wasn't satisfied, so I elected for closed-toe flats. My fingernails, on the other hand, turned out to be quite the pain in the butt. I'd never regretted biting my nails more in my life, and I frequently regretted biting my nails.

No matter how painted, pushed back, buffed, or evened out I tried to make them, they still looked like the hands of a neurotic wreck. And this carefree skinny white girl from Sweden or wherever could not look undone. I rummaged through my bathroom drawer for leftover press-on nails from eighth-grade graduation. The giant thumb-sized nails were all that was left of the set. No female's thumbs were that enormous. I sliced and shaped them into smaller fingernails; and after an hour of crafty manipulation, I had myself a full set. The glue had just about dried up, but it waited until the very last pinkie finger was pressed on to turn rock hard, which I took as a sign from Jesus.

I crawled into my bed around ten, but the anticipation of the next day made the clock tick slowly.

"Hey, Jesus?" I whispered into the darkness.

"Yeah?" he replied. I hadn't seen him appear, but there he was, sitting on the two-seater secondhand bench at the foot of my bed.

"Can you give me something to help me sleep?" I asked.

He laughed. "I'm not a pharmacist, Toya."

"But I'm so excited about tomorrow. Alex believes me! He's totally in on it," I told him.

"I saw that," said Jesus. "He's a cool kid. You're blessed to have him."

"Could I just stay like this for a while?"

"As you wish," he replied.

"It's even better than Christmas. Were you really born on that day, or was that just a guess? Oh crap, I shouldn't ask about things like that. Sorry, I shouldn't have said crap, either. Crap, I said it again." I couldn't understand why his smile made me want to cry.

"I've heard it all, child. I should get going, though; I have a few more lost sheep to find." He gently touched his index finger to my forehead.

GOOD-BYE, TOYA, AND GOOD RIDDANCE

If they could bottle whatever's in Jesus's index finger, crack would go out of business. I woke to a bright red bird chirping on my windowsill, and I ran to the bathroom mirror. As requested, the same white face from the day before cheesed back at me. I jumped in the shower with fruity Herbal Essences shampoo and conditioner in tow. After working up a good lather, I rinsed and repeated until my hair squeaked clean. The shampoo would've stripped every bit of moisture from my black hair, leaving each strand potato-chip dry. The pitiful conditioner wouldn't be nearly enough to replenish it.

I blew-brushed my locks dry, giving them a natural bump in less than five minutes. That five-minute bump would've taken an hour on black hair, if it were achievable at all.

For makeup, I drew little red targets on my cheeks with a tube of lipstick and rubbed. My old concealer worked fine for eye shadow, and I already had the mascara. *Cosmo* proved to be correct; brown mascara was way better. After pulling on my clothes, I looked like I belonged on the cover of one of those magazines.

Staring at the manifestation of my hopes and dreams, I questioned why God had done it for me. Surely everyone in Edgewood wanted something they didn't have, so why me? I studied myself for something extra special. Opened my mouth and peered down my throat for a spirit worthy of the grace of God. Some divine illumination to help make sense of my granted prayer, but aside from my beautiful new self, I didn't see anything specific. Only Toya stepping into white. Just then, Alex hauled himself from bed and into the bathroom.

"You still white?"

"Actually, yeah, I am. Jesus told me I could keep this look for a while," I replied.

"Cool." He dug at the inner corner of his eye. "We'll be popular yet, little sister. Now get out."

I tilted my head, wondering if God had visited him, too. How else could he believe me so blindly?

He loaded his toothbrush and then noticed I hadn't left. "What?" he asked, mouth overfilled with froth.

"Has Jesus come to you?"

He brushed vigorously and spit. "Not any more than usual."

"How . . . ," I said before losing my words. "I mean, why did you . . ." Again, the sentence fell apart. "I don't know." I gave up.

After a final gargle, he leaned against the bathroom counter. "I believe because I believe in you," he said with a depth and gravity I'd never heard. "That's it. Now . . ." He twisted me toward the door and gave me a push. "Get out."

"Toya!" Mom screamed. "Come on, you're making us late up there in your precious room!"

I shuffled downstairs and sat on the bottom step.

"Hey, sweet girl, you're ready for school early this morning," Dad said, just coming through the front door, gas station coffee in hand.

"I'm excited about school today. Where've you been so early?"

"I'm glad you asked. Hampton and I went for an early walk down to the car lot, and I've got my eye on a sharp gray Thunderbird. The Fiat has been acting funky lately, so I'm thinking rather than get it fixed, I should just buy another one. What do you think?" His eyes were saucers. My father never met a broke-down, clankity-clank, dusty vehicle he didn't love.

"I don't know, Dad. You have a few cars already; maybe we should just put some money in one of those, like the Volvo?" You'd think that at sixteen I would be smart enough to realize some things just are the way they are, but I couldn't fathom giving up on my dad. We looked strikingly similar. His eyes were my eyes. His nose was my nose. And Evilyn was right, his skin was my skin.

Well, all that was true when I was Toya.

"We'll discuss it, doll." He took a chockablock gulp from his coffee cup, spilled about a teaspoon's worth on the foyer floor, and walked away.

"Dad, seriously, you spilled your coffee," I said.

"I'll get it up in a bit," he replied, but I knew he wouldn't. For years, I'd been cleaning up after my dad.

"I heard you talking about some Thunderbird," Mom spat. "If you dare bring another half-piece of car into that driveway, I'll stuff you in the trunk and push you clean off Colossus."

Dad stared at Mom's eyes, and she gave a slight smile. I looked from his face to hers. They were smiling at each other!

"Uh . . . What's happening here?" I asked.

"Extraordinary things happen in Thunderbirds," he said, and then they laughed simultaneously.

Mom held her index finger in the air. "That doesn't mean buy it, though!"

Dad seized another mouthful from his mug.

"It's time, everybody, come on," she said, her dream-catcher earrings dangling from her ears. My mother looked gorgeous. She'd braided her hair into a soft crown and stuck a dollar-store flower pin in the back. No matter how little effort she'd put forth, she still managed to be the most beautiful woman in the world. Where the other mothers of Edgewood coveted a Mercedes and Louis Vuitton luggage, my mom preferred Joni Mitchell, freshly picked flowers, and long flowing things. Smooth tan skin, fluffy hair, and knocking on six foot tall, she could've been a model if she wasn't born in 1969 BOMBingham, Alabama.

Her tongue, on the other hand, could be lethal. Actually, only toward my dad; she was generally nice to everyone else. "What kind of man spills coffee on his own floor? Lord, help me. Every day, I have to deal with this."

See what I mean? I had never kissed a boy, but even I knew that the more you cut a man down, the less worthy he feels, and the more you suffer for it.

Alex strode down the stairs. "Let's blow this Popsicle stand." He wore a brand-new pair of Levi's we'd bartered down to seven quarters at an Edgewood yard sale. His shirt read *DAUGHTERS BEWARE!* in big black letters. "Like my shirt? Cool, huh?" he asked.

"Handsome, as usual," said Mom, grinning ear to ear.

"It was in the box marked 'free,'" Alex said. "Remember that yard sale, Toya?"

I nodded and smiled, even though he looked ridiculous. He truly was handsome, and I didn't understand why he wore a high-school-loser belt like me. He took after Mom: His skin was as light as a tanned white person's. His eyes were hazely and big, with long, shiny lashes. He stood six foot something, though he rarely stood up straight. Maybe it was because he wore shirts that said stupid stuff like *DAUGHTERS BEWARE!* on them, but I didn't have the heart to tell him any different.

The most popular senior guy in school, Josh Anderson, wasn't as handsome as Alex, but he had something my brother lacked: swag. It's the only way Bobby could marry Whitney; Billy Bob and Angelina, Arthur and Marilyn, and the list goes on. Some men had it—an untouchable, unexplainable aura that drew women like rednecks to the Iron Bowl.

"Got your homework?" asked Alex as we ducked into the backseat.

"Yep," I lied.

Alex narrowed his eyes and handed me a typed report entitled "Hester and Pearl, by Alex Williams." "Here you go."

I flipped through the first few pages. "Why are you giving me this?"

"I don't want you caught off guard when someone references Hester Prynne again." He smiled.

"Who, besides you, would reference Hester Prynne?"

Alex groaned. "At least read the character description in the back."

"How many times do I have to tell you to get this mirror fixed?" Mom started in on Dad. "And the pitiful air freshener..."

"Mom!" I yelled. "Stop being so mean!" Her nagging pricked me, too, not just Dad.

She didn't utter another word.

Post-sabbatical at Aunt Evilyn's, Mom had developed an acute case of child abandonment guilt. She knew Alex forgave her easily. He always had. But for my sake, my mother worked extra hard to get back into my good graces. Another daughter might have exploited it, but I was grateful that she cared so much what I thought of her. And I didn't want to contribute to her leaving again. The empty castle felt even emptier without her inside.

The Fiat didn't stall out once that morning, which was a good sign. As soon as Mom let up the seat, Alex and I jumped out, eager to start the day.

At drop-off, we stood on the curb, watching as our parents clanked off. "What's your new name?" Alex asked.

"Oh no. I forgot to come up with one." I almost flagged down the Fiat to take me back home.

Alex thumped my shoulder. "Don't worry, I've got you. How about Svetlana?"

"Svetlana sounds like a stripper name," I whispered.

"Okay, well, what about Elsa?"

"Better, but a little like an old housekeeper. Got anything, I don't know, cute?"

"Katarina?" he said.

"Ooh, that's it." I hugged him reflexively. It couldn't have lasted more than a second and a half, but by the time it was over, at least twenty sets of eyes ogled us. It must've been quite the sight, too—the eccentric black guy hugging the shiny new white girl. "What should we do?" I said in a hushed voice, nodding at gawking pass-ersby.

"Play it cool. I got this," he whispered back. Then he turned toward the crowd, held his arms open wide, and shouted, "She's . . . an . . . exchange . . . student. Her . . . name . . . is . . . Kat-a-riiiiiina." His voice cracked a little on the last part, so he gave up the floor. "Say . . . hello . . . Katarina!"

I gave a quick wave, hung my head, and walked into the principal's office. Alex and I called the principal's secretary, Ms. Wade, the Gatekeeper, since she wouldn't allow any student to see the principal unless they were near death, and even then it was debatable. We slowly approached the counter. "What can I do you for?" She didn't bother looking up from her JC Penney catalog.

"Uh, well, ma'am, I need to register an exchange student," announced Alex.

"Where from?" she said, not once diverting her eyes from the damn catalog.

"Kansas City, Kansas," I blurted, before Alex had a chance to say Sweden. I really didn't want to fake an accent for the rest of my life.

"Form's over there." She flicked her head toward a desk covered with stacks of papers. "Pink one."

The form was simple. Name, address, telephone number, how long you're planning to stay (which we left blank because God only knew), what you hope to learn while you're here, and other crap like that. We filled the lines with stuff they wanted to hear, like *I hope to learn why Alabama is the greatest place on Earth, how Montgomery overcame such adversity, and the power of nationwide democracy and patriotism blah blah blah.* In actuality, Montgomery had accomplished very little as far as I was concerned. Sure the buses were integrated—the Rosa Parks statue on the corner of South Jackson Street proved it—but racism was just as rampant as before; only cleverly hidden. We handed the application to the Gatekeeper.

"Grade?" she asked.

"Tenth." Since I'd nearly failed the tenth as Toya, I decided I might as well give it another shot.

She fumbled through a few files and pulled out a sample schedule. "Here are your classes." She picked up the JC Penney catalog and proceeded to ignore us. I liked JC Penney as much as the next red-blooded American, but come on, lady!

"All right, then, little sister," Alex whispered. "I have to go to class. Think you can handle this?"

"Yeah, I think so." I was so scared I could hardly breathe. I wouldn't see him until three o'clock. "I'll meet you right here after school?"

He nodded and walked away.

I watched him disappear, unable to move until he was completely out of sight. Looking over the schedule, I realized my first period was Alabama History with Mrs. Roseland, a sweet old Jewish woman who wore more red lipstick on her teeth and coffee cup than she did on her lips. I walked to her closed door and held my fist in the air for a good half a minute before working up the nerve to knock.

You are a strong girl. A strong, capable white girl.

"Coming, coming, coming," said Mrs. Roseland.

Last year, she offered Alex and me a ride home. It was raining, pouring, actually, and we'd barely made it off school grounds before the tornado sirens began howling. She pulled over to the side of the road, flung her passenger-side door open, and yelled for us to get in. She blasted Christmas tunes the majority of the ride home. I appreciated that she didn't show outward pity for the poor Williams siblings nearly sucked up by a tornado.

"Why are you listening to Christmas music?" Alex asked

before I poked him in his side. "Ow! I'm just saying. Aren't you Jewish? Ow!"

"Sorry, Mrs. Roseland," I said, eyeballing him. "Sometimes his curiosity gets the better of him."

"No, no, no need to apologize," she'd replied, yelling over the squeaking windshield wipers. She flipped her *Coexist* key chain and went into full history-teacher mode, explaining that most wars were initiated by minor religious differences. Then she transitioned with, "But to tell you the truth, I just love Christmas—the music, the ticker tapes, *The Santa Clause*, and back-to-back Will Ferrell dressed as an elf. It's just plain fun."

She chattered until we pulled into the empty castle's driveway. She'd simply given us the ride, bid us farewell, and never brought it up again. Mrs. Roseland was one of only a few teachers at Edgewood High that I genuinely liked.

The classroom door creaked open. "What can I do for you this morning, young lady?" she asked. She wore a frilly, knee-length red skirt paired with a crisp pink collared shirt and kitten heels. I'd never seen her wear the same outfit twice, but her look never veered too far from home base—splashy, vibrant color, and heels so low they may as well have been flats.

"I am an exchange student, Katarina from Kansas City." I used my own voice with an extra dash of exuberance.

"Kansas City, Missouri, or Kansas City, Kansas?" she asked, laughing at herself.

"Uhhh . . ."

"Oh. Oh. Oh. Class. Class. Class." Mrs. Roseland had a habit of saying certain words in threes. "Do we know where Kansas City is on the map?" She unrolled the giant map hanging from the ceiling.

Uh-oh.

"Katarina. Katarina. Katarina. Would you point out your lovely city for the class?"

Why the freaking hell did I choose Kansas? There were at least twenty-five middle states that I knew absolutely nothing about, and Kansas was one of them. Dwarfed by the map, those states were jumbled up in the Midwest or Mideast, above California, near Seattle, and the Grand Canyon, and/or Arizona, by the desert plains of Middle-earth. I focused until I finally saw rectangular Kansas located in the literal middle of the country. But no cities were labeled. I had no clue where to point.

My eyes closed automatically. "Jesus." I'd said it before I'd realized.

"Excuse me?" Mrs. Roseland replied. My eyes opened to Jesus standing behind Mrs. Roseland, pointing at tiny Kansas City on the giant wall-sized map. Everyone gawked at me, and no one paid any attention to the magical man standing at the head of the class. Clearly, no one else saw him. I went with it.

"Oh, no worries, I would be happy to." I curtsied. It just seemed appropriate to curtsy. Jesus's finger vanished milliseconds before my finger touched the map. "Oh, I see! Missouri and Kansas share Kansas City."

"Yes, yes, yes!" Mrs. Roseland gave me a round of applause like I had invented the Pythagorean theorem or something. "Most people don't realize this fact. They automatically think Kansas City must be in Kansas. People are so ill informed about the middle states."

"Ah, yes," I chuckled with her. "Oh, so very ill informed."

A handful of boys joined in her ovation. Their eyes stripped every inch of clothing right off my body. I'd waited for this moment since I was a little girl, to be desired, to be wanted, to be the center of attention for being anything other than a stumblebum.

Instead of enjoying it, I hurried to the first empty seat to make sure my headlights weren't penetrating my lace shirt. Of course, that would be impossible, since I'd pulled out the heavy-duty, big-titty bra. I'd bought it as a Halloween costume while thrifting with Mom a few years back. Titty-Head, a female superhero who soared through the air with the help of her trusty pink cape and big-titty bra. That Halloween, I locked myself in my room and jogged figure eights around my bed, never revealing Titty-Head to anyone, not even Alex. I think I was going through some type of rebellion that year. Edgewood could do that to a girl, especially a black one.

I'd never felt so many eyes focused on me. Even when I closed my eyes for long blinks, I felt them. So many eyes. Eyes studying my eyes. Eyes sizing up my clothes. Eyes checking out my shoes. Eyeballing my big-titty bra. Eyes every freaking where. Even Mrs. Roseland's smiling eyes scrutinized me. I liked Mrs. Roseland, but damn. I chalked it up to some sort of new-girl disease and told myself it would subside after a few days. Plus, Jesus would surely be disappointed if I complained on the second day. Really, though, it wasn't Jesus who scared me. It was his dad. In the Sunday school picture Bible, he looked like Zeus on the mountaintop, searching for some ungrateful maggot to strike down. I didn't want to be that maggot, so I kept my trap shut.

Mrs. Roseland went on for an hour about the fighting tarpon, Alabama's state saltwater fish. Every few sentences she paused and said, "Anybody want to add anything? Anybody? Anybody? Anybody?" Crickets chirped in return. After the fourth effort, I felt sorry for her, but I couldn't afford to raise my hand, seeing that I was technically visiting from Kansas/Missouri, and I shouldn't know diddly about the state fish.

When Mrs. Roseland turned her back, a crooked paper airplane sailed across the room, poked me in the shoulder blade, and landed nose-first in the cleavage of my big-titty bra. When

Raymond Neily smirked and avoided eye contact, I knew who had thrown it. Dumbass. And I don't use the word *dumbass* lightly; he really was, truly, in every sense of the word, a dumbass. Halfway through seventh grade, he taped a KICK MY BROTHER sign on my backpack, and vice versa on Alex's. I saw Alex's first and then he saw mine. That was the singular event that turned the tides for us. We went from regular kids to school jesters and never quite lived it down. Still, I couldn't resist. I unfolded the airplane.

Nice tits

See what I mean? The worst part was he probably thought it was a compliment.

Should I ball it up and throw it back? Or would a white chick dig that type of stuff?

Jesus?

No, I needed to handle this on my own. I refolded the airplane and shot it in his direction. Unfortunately for me, it hit an innocent redhead in the eyelid. "Hey!"

But the class was over and I was saved by the bell. Well, not a bell exactly: After an extensive case study in human behavior, the Montgomery County Board of Education installed ocean sounds in the place of bells. They were supposed to be calming but didn't change the frenzy in the hallways as far as I could tell. Just another inessential ornament to spend their money on.

I quickly gathered my things to scuttle out the door.

"'Ey!" Deanté yelled after me. "'Ey! 'Ey!"

I hurried along, pretending not to hear him.

The halls filled quickly. Waves of teenagers crisscrossed one another to get to their classes, a synchronized dance. The only thing out of place was me. The seas parted on my approach. Girlfriends elbowed boyfriends, cheerleaders looked at their feet. Football players, dance girls, flag girls, even mathletes hushed in my presence. It was like the first scene of *The Lion King*, when the entire forest of African animals travel to catch a glimpse of Simba's birth.

> *From the day she arrived at our high school,*
> *Her big-titty bra stepped into the sun,*
> *There's more to see than could ever be seen,*
> *More to do than could ever be done.*

But it wasn't Simba or Toya, it was Katarina who was parting the Edgewood seas, reshuffling the circle of life, finally ruling the school. No, not Katarina. Me.

And for the first time in my life, I felt powerful.

KATARINA ASCENDING

That was it: The door slammed on Toya, and Katarina emerged the victorious one. The hallway was a pressure cooker of emotion. Enthusiasm and horniness from the boys, fear and anger from the girls. I straightened my spine until it hurt; *America's Next Top Model* judges said that the less comfortable you felt, the better you looked. So be it. Familiar eyes pored over me, but instead of avoiding the stares, I now bathed in them.

I deliberately dropped my mechanical pencil. "Oh!" I said. Everyone stopped. Everyone! I bent down slowly, tooting my butt into the air to retrieve it. Mid-bend, the ocean waves stopped swooshing over the intercom, yet no one scrambled for class. Only silence. Stillness. Control.

I picked up the pencil and went on to my next class, and so did everyone else.

My remaining classes brought more of the same. That day produced two more folded notes from guys, more eye rolls from girls than I could count, and an invitation to join the show choir without even trying out. The frilly note had been slipped through the slits of my locker, and it was marked *Confidential* in big red letters. The eye rolls made me feel triumphant. The fact that I could evoke visceral expressions of angst from rich white girls put a little extra pep in my step. The show choir invite, on the other hand, pissed me off. Toya had tried out for show choir three times and never made it. How was that fair?

"Hey, Katarina! Wait up!" I stopped at the sound of Alex's voice.

"Alex, hey," I whispered. "Let's go over here by the lockers." I led him from the hallway to a more secluded alcove.

"Why are we whispering?"

"No reason," I said. "Just don't want too many people asking questions. That's all."

"Makes sense," he said, matching my whisper. "You holding up okay?"

"Yeah, I'm great, actually."

"Okay, just checking in. I want the play-by-play. See you at three."

Swim was my next and final class. As Toya, I'd never once dressed out for swim class. You'd think white people would see that black people dominate every sport with one glaring exception—swimming. Why? Aunt Evilyn would say, *Cuckabugs and chlorine should never live in the same place.* She was absolutely right about that one. Also, ethnic butts burst out of swimsuit bottoms. Ask any black female over the age of twelve what's on her mind when she's wearing a swimsuit; if she answers honestly, she'll say her rear end. Some smart entrepreneur should invent ethnic bathing suits and chlorine substitute so blacks can finally take the sport of swimming from white people.

But I didn't have to worry about such nonsense any longer. Our swim teacher, Miss Baker, offered me a loaner suit. After stepping out of the stall, I could hear a pin drop in the locker room. The high-cut bright red one-piece made me look like a younger *Baywatch* babe. Usually that locker room was every boy's fantasy, nakedness all over the place. But that day, even the cutest girls with the tightest butts kept their towels firmly shut until they reached the pool. I, on the other hand, deserted my towel and switched my skinny hips to the edge of the water. I danced a big toe on the surface, teasing my crowd. Finally, I sat on the rim, arched my back, and slid in slowly. I reveled in the floating sensation. I'd never actually allowed my hair into any body of water other than the bathtub.

I took a deep breath and lowered myself underwater. Black skin was filled with so many barriers, so many restrictions, so many. Don't walk too deep into that neighborhood. Stop and turn around if you see too many Confederate flags catching wind on front porches. Don't you get in that chlorine water, or you'll mess up your perm. Don't talk too proper or you'll be accused of talking white. Don't talk too Ebonic or you'll be accused of talking ghetto. I started to run out of air, but I held it long enough to see feet dangling, bodies flipping, hands flapping upward and downward. Such freedom. Such fun. I would've cried if I weren't underwater. I surfaced to smooth my hair back, and rose out slow like a mermaid.

"Hi there." I knew who that voice belonged to. I had mini-stalked him a few years back. Eighteen-year-old Josh Anderson.

I smiled mysteriously, or tried to anyway. "Hello."

"You're new here?" He was close enough to inhale. He smelled like chlorine and Acqua Di Gio cologne. What did I smell like? Damn it, I hoped not diesel fuel.

"I'm an exchange student." I pointed to myself with both thumbs. "Katarina." Stupid!

"Nice to meet you, Katarina. I'm Josh." He held his hand out to shake. So sexy and mature. I shook, careful not to grab too firmly. Delicate as a flower was the impression I wanted to leave him with. "Where are you from?"

"Kansas City, right on the line of Kansas and Missouri. Most people don't know that." I giggled. Double stupid!

"I knew that." He flicked his neck to force the hair from his face. "Kansas City Chiefs did okay last year. You been to any games?"

I cleared my throat and stood a little straighter. "Of course, who hasn't?" I slapped him hard on the shoulder, too hard. "Sorry." Triple stupid!

"No worries." He stepped back, peeled his T-shirt off, and dove splash-free into the pool, like the water was his home. He swam a full two lengths before I had the power to look away. When I did, I sashayed to the bleachers.

"Do you know who just talked to you?" asked Amera Bailey, the second most popular girl in the tenth grade only after her best friend and twin, Amelia.

Yes, of course I knew. "No, who?"

"That"—she placed her skinny arm around my waist—"was *the* Josh Anderson."

Amelia appeared out of nowhere. "The oldest son of *the* Andersons; owners of Anderson Toyota, Jeep, Dodge. He drives, like, a different new car every day."

"He gave his last girlfriend a Prius for Christmas, and he is so nice that when he dumped her, he never even asked for it back," said Amera.

"Why did they break up?" I asked, but I already knew. His last girlfriend was named Ashley Hemphill. Rumor had it that she had a little sex problem: She liked doing it—a lot. And, apparently, one guy wasn't enough.

"I'm not one to gossip, but . . . ," said Amera.

I hated when people set up their sentences with "I'm not one to gossip, but." You may as well announce to the world that you're a low-down dirty big mouth who likes talking crap about everyone, including whoever you're talking crap to right now. "Her name is Ashley Hemphill, but her nickname is Humphill, if you know what I mean." They laughed in tandem.

Amelia picked up where the other one left off. "Nobody likes her, really. Like, everyone just put up with her when she was dating Josh. I heard she has the gonorrhea." *The gonorrhea.* She said it like Ashley was possessed by a demon named Gonorrhea.

"We like you," they said at exactly the same time.

"I'm Amera."

"And I'm Amelia."

I pointed to myself. "Katarina." I had two friends on my first day, more than I'd made in two full years at Edgewood High as a black girl, and they were popular ones to boot.

The ocean waves whooshed, announcing the end of school.

79

Amera and Amelia grabbed their identical pink-and-green Vera Bradley backpacks. "Hey, what family are you staying with?"

Crap. "The Williams family." My eyes dropped to my knees.

"That black family with the fitted sheets hanging in the place of curtains?" Amera uncrossed her legs at the knee and recrossed them at the ankle.

Amelia said, "OMG, you have to *live* with that loser Toya and her spazz of a brother?"

"What agency would place a girl like you with niggers?" Their eyes widened in shock, and then flickered with anger.

They'd said it together.

I don't know why I was shocked.

I knew for sure that Montgomery white people used that word in the comfort of their own homes and country clubs.

Just.

Hearing it.

Out loud.

Was.

Quite.

Hurtful.

I'd only heard the word spoken once before. When I was in kindergarten, a pigtailed little girl called me by that name. I didn't know what it meant, I just knew that it stung worse than a yellow jacket. When I told Aunt Evilyn, she said, *Get used to it, little girl. I was called a nigger so much as a child, I thought it was my name.*

"What's wrong, Kat?" one of them asked. I don't even know which. "You never heard 'nigger' before?"

"Of course she hasn't. She's from . . . Where are you from again?"

"Um . . . Kansas City." I couldn't look up from my knocking knees. The twins wore the same baby-blue polish on their toenails.

"She's from the North, stupid. They were part of the group that invaded the Confederacy. They don't say nigger up there anymore."

"I could not imagine. You need a ride home, Kat? That black family's car smells like a junkyard. That can't be safe for your lungs."

"Our daddy bought us a convertible Bug for our sixteenth. We'll take you to the black people's house if you want."

I nodded, still speechless. They had just called me a nigger and a loser; well, they called Toya a nigger and a loser, but still.

All the way home they talked about this person and that person, the kind of insults that should draw pity rather than laughter. For instance, Amera called a guy retarded—worst part was, the guy she called retarded truly had Down syndrome. Jim was the sweetest, gentlest soul walking the halls of Edgewood High.

Amelia, not to be outdone by her sister, said Tina Dillard had a lazy eye because her dad beat her. I didn't say a word, just laughed along like a sheep.

We reached my driveway. "Ew, what the hell kind of dog is that? It looks like it has the mange."

"Thanks for the ride." I shut the door, and Hampton let out a low growl in the direction of the twins.

"Hey, Kat?" Amelia rolled down the passenger-side window. "The dance team is having a party for the new recruits this Saturday night. Josh will be there. You in?"

I nodded enthusiastically to the two girls who'd called me, my brother, my mother, and my father niggers. For a fleeting moment, my guts hit the driveway.

"You text?" asked Amera.

"I don't have a cell phone, sorry." I shrugged.

"They didn't even give you a cell?" They were outraged. "We'll tell you about it in swim, see you tomorrow."

When I opened the door, I realized that I had forgotten something, something big.

Alex.

GOOD THINGS FALL APART ALL THE TIME

By the time Alex walked through the front door, the sun was gone and the *Unsolved Mysteries* closing credits were rolling. I jumped up to meet him.

"I waited for an hour. Then I looked for you. I screamed into the girls' bathrooms like a pervert. A freshman girl called me one!"

"I'm sorry," I said, knowing it wasn't nearly enough.

"Who brought you here? Did they have air-conditioning?" He focused on the strangest things when he got his feelings hurt.

"The twins."

He looked at me like I had snakes crawling on my head. "They hate us!" He was right. Or he was almost right; they hated Toya and Alex, not Katarina. He shuffled up the stairs. When he reached the top, he yelled, "And I found quarters on the way home! Enough to afford a whole meal. That I ate! By myself!" And he slammed the door.

When he reopened the door, I hoped for his change of heart. "Mom!" he yelled. "Did I get any mail?"

"Not today," she yelled back from the living room.

And he slammed the door again.

Most girls despised their big brothers, but not me. Alex and I were the best of friends. When our parents went rolling off the deep end, we held on to each other for dear life. My brother and I had rarely fought. Sure, we argued over McChicken quantities, and who got the front seat, but never about anything of substance. I ached for both of us. For him because he was alone, and for me, because I couldn't fully enjoy success unless he succeeded, too.

Earlier that day, I had not thought twice about his feelings. To be honest, I forgot him completely. I was free of him—of us—for the first time, and it felt magnificent. However, when he walked into that house, sweaty and exhausted, my heart dropped and splattered on the hardwood with my dad's spilled coffee. Yesterday, I imagined I loved my brother more than I loved myself. Today, I wasn't so sure.

"You're fighting the members of your own army, you know." Mom sat in the dark, listening. She recycled about twelve parables that she made to fit every life situation. "What's going on with you two?"

"Some girlfriends brought me home, and I forgot Alex," I said.

"I gathered that much from the argument; I meant what's the real issue? You two never fight." She sounded almost wounded by the thought of us fighting.

I sat on a pillow next to her. "Everybody fights, Mom." I wanted to ask her what she expected us to do with two parents who fought more than they breathed.

"That's not true. Some human beings are put on Earth for one another. When your father and I brought you home, Alex looked at you like you were God's screaming little miracle. I would say that he protected you, but even then you had a symbiotic relationship." She had been watching National Geographic Channel, and she'd picked up science words.

"You looked out for each other. Alex was mischievous. He needed discipline, but you wouldn't have it. Whenever he was in trouble, you wobbled in front of him—Pampers and all—as his human shield." She paused. "You love each other, Latoya."

"Like you and Evilyn?" I asked, my voice thick with sarcasm.

"Latoya Williams, you watch your tongue about your auntie," she answered with a touch of rage. "You don't know as much as you think you do, child."

I began to apologize. "Mom—"

"I'm not the best mother. I've never put on that I am. . . ."

"Mom . . . I'm—"

She held her hand up to stop me from talking. "But I'm here now. And if you never listen to me again in life, listen to me now. Never abandon your big brother." Mom lifted herself from the pillows and walked toward her room—head down.

"I hear you, Mom," I said after her. I really was listening, but was I supposed to put my life on hold for him? How were either of us going to grow up with a Velcro sibling? I was doing him a favor. I was like the mother bird that throws her chicks from a tree to teach them to fly. I had never seen one plummet and splat. They all figured it out halfway down and then ascended toward the clouds. Alex would be just fine.

The following morning seemed the same as any other, only different. Dad spilled the coffee in the foyer, Mom screamed bloody murder, and we all jammed into the Fiat. But Alex was different. He wore black from head to toe. Even his mismatched socks were black; one was a faded ankle riser and the other more of a stocking. The whites of his eyes were red and veined, his shoulders curved forward, and he didn't look my way once. He was a brother in mourning.

When we pulled up to school, he hung back and let me walk ahead. Eyes still beat down on me, but today they turned up at the corners—smiling.

"Hi, Kat," chirped a random freshman cheerleader.

"OMG. You look so supercute," squeaked another one.

Instinctively, I checked for Alex. He was already gone.

"Hey, pretty girl." Amera hooked on to my right arm.

"You have Mrs. Roseland first period?" Amelia hooked on to the left.

"How did you—"

"People talk. Let's skip." They grinned identical grins and led me to the bleachers lining the practice football field. They yapped on about the less popular kids. While they gossiped, I thought about how Alex still saw the same old Toya with the hair, and the skin, and the nose. I realized how excruciating that must've been for him. I was his best friend, and completely unreachable.

"Hey, Kat, Josh is totally digging you." Amera snapped me out of it.

"Digging me?" I sat up a little straighter.

"Totally," said Amelia. "I texted Stephen last night. He's been Josh's BFF since, like, kindey. He texted that Josh would not shut up about the sexy new exchange student. He said that he was going to ask that loser Alex about you, but I texted him *never* to talk to that guy in public or else."

"Or else what?" I wanted to hear it from her mouth.

She laughed. "Stephen is a ginger, not a babe like Josh. But he's just as popular, so I let him rub on my boobs sometimes."

Amera added, "If Stephen goes around talking to losers, he's deducted popularity points."

"Guys like Josh can talk to whoever they want. Stephen can't, and if he does . . ."

"No more boobies . . ."

"And all guys really want to do is to touch boobs." Amelia bent in and whispered, "I let him kiss my nipple once."

Amera punched her arm. "Why do you always have to one-up me?" They bickered about breasts, boys, and popularity until the ocean whooshed. We made it back in time for second period, kissed the air twice, and went our separate ways. I paid no attention in my next three classes, and I even dozed in Barnhouse's biology.

Mr. Barnhouse was a staple in Edgewood culture. Old, white-headed, monotone, and utterly predictable; teaching the same material year after year. The cell cycle project, and A through D bubble quizzes. About a decade back, some senior made up a Barn-house bubble quiz cheat song using penis mnemonics for all eight twenty-five-question tests. The first quiz mnemonics were *Big Cokes* (only he didn't say cokes) *Big Cokes Ass Cokes Big Ducks* (only he didn't say ducks) *Ducks Cokes Ducks Big Ass Cokes And Ducks All Cokes And All Ducks And Asses Are A+*. Needless to say, all Barnhouse biology students since then scored straight As. Excluding Toya, who didn't do well in any subject. I'd always considered myself a smart girl— school just wasn't made for people like me.

One day when Mom let me stay home from school, I half watched *The View* where Whoopi Goldberg said structured education wasn't for her, either. Instead, her awesome mother let her spend those hours at the library learning on her own. I think that's a testament to high school simply not being for everyone, especially offbeat black girls like Whoopi and me. I'd take eight hours in the library any day if it meant avoiding these wannabe bozos. Of course, Katarina was now the reigning queen of wannabe bozos, but what the hell, right?

During bio, my wondering how Alex's day was going was pushed aside by thoughts of Josh. He'd spoken to me once while I was still Toya. It could be considered a conversation, because he said something, and I said something back, and then he said something in response to what I said. I'll never forget the tingles I felt. I'd looked behind me to make sure no one cooler was standing there—there'd been only me. He stared into my eyes, smiled slightly, and asked for the honey mustard. Yeah, it sounds stupid now, but back then it *meant* something.

After bio, I went to the choir room to accept Mr. Holder's phantom invitation to join show choir. I'd met him before as a member of girls' choir, which fell dead last in the hierarchy of Edgewood choral groups. Girls' choir was like show choir's less attractive, less talented, mousy-brown little sister; or the gloomy girl who carries the flag at the tail end of the Christmas parade.

The door to the choir room was cracked open, and Mr. Holder sat behind the shiny grand piano, rumbling off Rach 3 like it was "Twinkle, Twinkle, Little Star." His eyes were closed, and he was completely lost in his art, so I watched. The man was a master.

"Oh dear God, have I died and gone to the heavenly heavens?" Mr. Holder opened his eyes and jumped up, sending the bench to the ground with a loud crash.

I jumped, too, since Mr. Holder hadn't spoken two words to me as Toya. "I didn't mean to disturb you...."

He cupped his palm around my chin. "Feel absolutely free to disturb me anytime, you lovely thing." He grabbed my hands and forced two twirls. "Dare I say, little madam, you are the most beautiful vision I've seen to grace these halls in years—maybe decades." I felt my cheeks flame. "Would you do me the honor of joining my magnificent chorus?"

"Do you want me to try out?" I asked.

He winked. "Ahhh, why yes, of course. General tryouts are next Tuesday, but I don't see any reason why we can't go ahead and get them done right now." He plopped back down on the piano bench and pressed a single note. "Give me an ahhhhhhhhh."

"Ahhhhhhhhhh."

"Brilliant! You're hired!"

"Excuse me, sir, but you've only just met me. Why would I qualify for show choir without trying out?"

"See! This is why I like you." He slipped his arm around my shoulder and led me into his office. "You're beautiful, humble, and inquisitive. Have a seat."

I sat on the white leather couch near the rear of his office. He sat next to me and grabbed my hand. "Can I share the key to success with you? Young... what's your name?"

"Katarina."

"Ha! Perfect, yes, Katarina. The key to success in Montgomery, Alabama, is the perfect balance of aesthetic beauty and genuine talent. Visualize this: the most dynamic group of singers, hitting every note to masterful perfection. Close your eyes. Tell me, what do you see?"

"Uhhh..."

"I'll give you a hint, they're up there with the good Lord Almighty," he said.

"Clouds?"

"Starts with an 'A,' and ends with 'gels.'"

"Oh... angels."

"Ha! What are they wearing?" He shot to his feet. "No, no, keep your eyes shut. Tell me."

"I don't know, robes."

"What color is their hair?" I could feel him pacing now.

"All of them?" I replied.

"All of them."

"Jesus wouldn't let all of his angels have the same hair," I said, quite sure of myself. Jesus would want variety in his angels.

"And just when was the last time you spoke to Jesus?" he chuckled.

"Uhhhh . . . ," I said, squinting through one eye.

He interrupted. "Close 'em!"

I tried to envision my version of heaven, but there wasn't a complete picture there. Only fragments of my everyday life—Hampton chasing off Alabama Power, Dad taking an afternoon walk, Mom tucking a flower in her crown, Alex and Toya conquering Colossus. I knew that Mr. Holder expected an idyllic wonderland with naked pink-cheeked cherubs shooting arrows at fluffy rain clouds, but when I closed my eyes, I saw the inhabitants of the empty castle.

"The answer is platinum blond," he bellowed. "Are there any fat ones? No. Any with bad teeth? None. Any with psoriasis?"

"What's pso—"

"Never mind." He sat beside me again. "I think you get the point now. I don't give two puppy poots if you can sing or not. I just need you front row center." He held his hands in front of him, thumbs together, framing me. "You're perfect. Would you be my Dolly P.?" He bent to his knee.

I couldn't help smiling. He would make for a classic cartoon character as the brazen, overly dramatic, chubby music teacher. "I will," I said, even though I had no idea what he meant by Dolly P.

FUDGE!

Lunch period drew nearer. Since Alex's lunch was a half hour before mine, I always ate lunch alone as Toya, which is every teenager's worst nightmare. I'd pre-line my pockets with napkins, stuff chicken fingers in when nobody was looking, and eat in a bathroom stall. Mostly, it worked fine until someone pooped. The mother of all appetite stealers—someone pushing a turd when you're trying to eat a pecan brownie. But now I had the twins. They were bitches, but their company beat eating in the bathroom. I spotted them at the Chosen Table.

The table was located underneath a wall-sized mural of our mascot, the Trojans. The advanced art class had painted the wall as a final project a few years ago. It was breathtaking—three beefy white men wearing long red robes, breastplates, and broom helmets. They guarded the lunchroom, holding on to bronze shields and swords, but the majority of their attention was reserved for the Chosen Table. One of the three Trojans pointed his sausage-sized index finger at the only booth-style table in the lunchroom. It had become an unwritten rule that only the popular kids sat there, and I was on my way. I quickly snaked around the other tables.

"Hi, guys." I bent forward to kiss the air and squished into the crimson booth. "I just got a secret invite into show choir."

"Omigosh, Kat, you're the total package now," said Amera.

"Show choir at Edgewood isn't for dorks and losers like at your old school, probably. Only the hottest of the hot get invited into ours," said Amelia, examining her nails.

"Tryouts are a total sham. Amelia and I got invited to skip girls' choir and join show freshman year...."

"Yeah, we split the front-row-center spot every season," said Amelia.

"Because we're the hottest," Amera added. "Where will Mr. Holder put you, I wonder?"

Sensing confrontation, my stomach clenched and let out a hungry noise. "Those chicken fingers look delish. Either of you want anything?" I stood, noticing their empty trays.

They looked at each other, then back at me. "You can't eat

chicken fingers." One creepy monotone voice came out of both of them.

"Why not?" I attempted to hide my disappointment. "What's wrong with the chicken fingers?"

"Have a seat, Kitty-Kat." Wow, they never even asked if they could rename me Kat, and now this.

"Don't take this the wrong way or anything. . . ."

"But people are talking. . . ."

"They say you're hot and everything, but . . ."

"You're kind of . . ."

"Fat," they said the final word together. *Fat.* There's a word I had never been called before—to my knowledge.

"I'm a size six," I said slowly, to make sure they understood.

They laughed like I'd made a joke. "Six is fat, Kat," said Amera. "And we can't hang with fat people. You want to aim for two or less."

"I'm double zero," boasted Amelia.

"Show-off!" Amera said. "I'm a regular zero."

"Anyway." Amelia turned her attention back to me. "If you eat, which you probably shouldn't, eat lettuce or something like that."

So there was a downside to whiteness after all. Starvation. I had never tried starvation. Huge school lunches and whatever fast food Alex and I could scrounge up for dinner kept my stomach from snarling. To Dad's credit, he slipped us Nutty Buddies and Pecan Swirls to supplement the black-eyeds, so Alex and I had bed-time snacks. Amera and Amelia were walking skeletons. Shadowy around the eyes, sunken cheeks, gaunt even. Dancing at around ninety pounds, give or take.

The lingering black girl within did not approve of the twins' protruding collarbones and empty plates. In the black community, someone's Big Mama would've jacked their mouths open and forced sweet potato pie down their throats like baby birds. That's one thing I'd always appreciated about black women. They ate what-ever the heck they wanted, and black men loved them for it. Before she died, my grandmother would host Sunday dinners of ham-hock-soaked collard greens with buttermilk cornbread cut into squares and stacked into mini mountains. Oxtails dripping with brown gravy seated on a bed of fluffy white rice. And, for the spe-cialest of special occasions, chitterlings.

"How do you both stay so skinny?" I felt like I had to yell over my growling stomach.

"We have different methods. I enjoy food, so I eat it and just throw it back up again—" said Amelia.

Amera interrupted. "I think that's disgusting and it screws up your teeth. So I just watch what I eat."

"By watch what she eats, she means leaves of lettuce and the occasional apple," said Amelia.

They discussed their diseases like a sportscaster discussed golf. There were people out there with cancer, diabetes—real stuff that can't be cured—but their cure was four quarters away in a McDonald's drive-through. If they weren't so awful, I would've felt bad for them.

But I needed someone to sit with. Plus, I'd always wondered what it felt like to eat at the Chosen Table.

"Okay, I won't eat, then." I folded my arms into a tight wad.

The next two periods came and went slow as Christmas. I counted stomach growls to pass the time. Fifty-two. One after the other after the other. Then dread set in. Yes, I was hungry, but that wasn't why—it was the thought of Alex and our quarter game. That game wasn't a game at all; it was our way of avoiding situations like these. Alex would be so disappointed that I'd stooped to this level for something as ridiculous as fitting in with the twins. In that moment, I reviled who I'd become.

After dressing out for swim, I took a seat on the bleachers next to the twins and shut my eyes.

"I heard that your stomach talked more in class than the teacher," said Amelia.

"That's a good sign, you know. It means the fat is dying in your gut," Amera added. What a stupid girl. "It will pass, Kitty-Kat, we promise."

"And afterward, you'll be supermodel skinny for yearbook pics."

My eyes eased open. "How much weight will I lose?" I asked. My evil aunt Evilyn already said I had chicken legs. She would surely label me a crack addict if I lost another ounce.

Amelia picked at her nails. "You could lose, like, ten pounds in a week. You can go from pudgy to super skinny. Just like us."

"Whoa, check out Josh." Amera pointed to the second lane of the pool. As he lifted himself from the water, every vein in his forearms bulged to lift the weight of his lean wet body. His hair stuck to his head until he shook it free into wavy blond chunks. His gaze found me.

ME.

The twins elbowed me hard in the ribs just like Alex used to do. I waved my fingers in the air and batted my new eyelashes. That moment made me think of my favorite movie in the world, *Sabrina*. It's about the dorky chauffeur's daughter's transition into a beautiful object of desire. Granted, the parallels were limited. Sabrina was still Sabrina when she became special—I had to become something else entirely. And Sabrina never abandoned her brother for starving doublemint racists; then again she didn't have a brother, so who knows what she would have done.

"Hello again." He left his shirt off and drank down the attention. For the first time I realized nothing was less attractive than a guy who knew he was attractive. Plus, I was so hungry that Ian Somerhalder would've annoyed me in that moment. From far off, Josh looked like he'd been carved from ivory and placed at Edgewood High as a relic to show other guys what they were supposed to look like. Now that I saw him, I saw his eyes—the eyes of the arrogant, the pompous, and the ugly. Not physically ugly—uglier than that.

God had gifted me with an impeccable judge of character, and I knew then that my longtime crush was a jerk for sure. The twins were, too, but what the hell. I caught Josh's eyes darting to my boobs more than twice. It looked like the twins were right about boys and their passion for breasts. Strike three. Blame the hunger or my intuition; either way I knew in that moment that I was done with Josh. I leaned my head back and disregarded him. He could look at my chest all he wanted as long as I didn't have to look into those cold eyes.

"Kat, Josh is trying to talk to you." One of the twins shook my arm.

"She's not from Alabama, you know. Their rules are different up north." They sounded so similar that it was impossible to tell who was speaking. Really, though, I didn't care. Hunger was making me very, very impatient.

"Whatever, dude." I listened to his wet feet pad off.

"And just what the hell was that?" asked Amera, I think. My eyes were still closed. "You dissed the sexiest guy in the whole school."

"He was staring at my boobs, and he wasn't even trying to hide it." I didn't bother opening my eyes.

"That's what guys do! We've discussed this."

"So lame, Kat."

"Well, he had a booger on his nose. Sorry, girls, but that's not sexy in any state." I could sense their disgust. Want to gross a girl out? Talk about snot, boogers, or loogies. Alex was a gross-out genius. He'd developed the snot rocket to end all arguments. I smiled at the memory, and then the thought made me sad.

The ocean sounded. "Ugh, whatever. Want to go to Gus Von March after school?"

"Hey!" One of them shook my thigh. When I opened my eyes, I realized that it was Amera. "Omigosh, what's wrong with you? You're being a total bitch."

"Yeah," said Amelia.

"We took you in, and, like, do you know how many girls would kill to trade places with you?"

"Yeah!"

"Stop saying that, Amelia!"

"What? I'm agreeing with you, idiot."

"Well, stop it. You sound like a parrot."

"Screw you!"

"No, screw you!"

"Go to hell!"

"You're stupid!"

"Stop doing that!"

"No! You stop!"

"Shut up!"

"Just . . . shut . . . up . . . Omigosh!" they said. Afterward, they both looked over at me and laughed—I couldn't bring myself to join them. I may have thought it was cute or cool a couple of days ago, but not today. Today they were just buttholes.

"Come on, Kat. We're going to show you the best store ever."

GUS VON MARCH REBOOTED

I paused at the entrance, remembering my big brother and me in the same store just days earlier.

"Come on in, Kat."

"Isn't it beautiful?" Amera grabbed my hand and pulled me toward the flowery pink-and-green Lily Pulitzer display to the right of the entrance.

Amelia held a pleated seersucker miniskirt covered in flowers up to my waist. "It's just seventy dollars. What do you think?"

"Cute skirt," I said, but it was easily the most ridiculous thing I'd ever seen. It belonged on a toddler on Easter Sunday. Seventy dollars, *pssshhhha!*

"Skort," they replied. "It's a skirt and shorts combined."

"They're all the rage at Edgewood. We don't have to obey the fingertip-length skirt rule when it's shorts, too."

"Omigosh!" Amera lifted the matching tank top to my chest and pulled me to the floor-length mirror. "This will totally make you look like you're from Alabama."

"Totally!"

"Stop that!"

"You stop that!"

"Ughhhhhhh!"

"I like it," I said without smiling. Really, I hated it, and Alex would've agreed immediately.

"Omigosh, I knew you would love it. Try it on."

"Yeah, and take this with you." Amelia tossed me an eighty-dollar water bra. "That will help fill out the top."

"I'm already a D cup. How big do you want them to be?" I asked.

"Why settle for D?"

"When you can be an E..."

"Or F..."

"When you can be a G..." They bumped hip bones and smacked me on the butt as I entered the corner dressing room.

Mirrors covered all three walls of the fitting room. My bare feet sank into the plush pink carpet. The tiny crack in the leftmost mirror and daisy-shaped stain on the bench jogged my memory of the day I'd tried on swimsuits in that very space as Toya. That day, I scrutinized my naked figure from all angles and began crying wildly. At one point, an employee quietly asked if I was all right. I sniffled in return, and she cleared the rest of the rooms.

"We've all been there, little miss. No such thing as a body looks good in three inches of cloth." Her twang was deep and sweet—more of a calm New Orleans sound than classic Montgomery false. "Is there anything I can do for you?"

"I want my brother," I said through snivels. *Beep, beep, beep!!!* My big brother was there to talk me off the ledge.

I jumped at the loud knock on the door. "Kat, come on. We're dying to check you out."

"Here I come."

Two minutes later, I looked like a Southern Baptist blow-up doll.

"Omigosh, Kat, you *have* to get that outfit," said Amera.

Amelia cupped her hands around my waist. "It makes you look so much skinnier; you totally have to get this."

I glanced at the price tag hanging underneath my armpit. "A hundred and seventy dollars."

"The blacks didn't give you spending money?"

I shrugged, and they shot a quick look at each other—judgment. "Take it off and we'll get our makeup done."

"We know the Lancôme lady."

"Shit," I said under my breath.

"What?" they said.

"Oh, nothing."

When I finally exited the room, the twins were already seated in the makeup high chair. The same Lancôme lady that Alex and I had fought applied liquid liner to Amera as Amelia watched, arms folded.

"Kat! You can be next." Amera motioned me toward the counter—her eyes still half-closed. Amelia refolded her arms and let out a hostile sigh. "Amelia. Be patient, my God. You are such a brat. Ouch!"

"I'm so sorry," said the Lancôme lady.

Amera held her palm to her left eye. "You poked me in the eye with the liquid liner, seriously, bitch!"

"I am so sorry," she said again, staring as I approached the counter. "Hi, I mean, where's your boyfr—?" She bumped a small blush display, and it went crashing to the floor.

"Lucy! What the hell is wrong with you?" the twins yelled.

Lucy was on her knees, attempting to clean the broken blush from the marble-ish floor, but she was only making it worse— swirling the pinks into the violets, creating a tie-dye effect. Her head was down, and she kept mumbling, "I'm sorry, I'm sorry, I'm sorry, I'm sorry . . ."

"She'll be all right. Her eye needed a good poke," Amelia snickered.

"Shut up, stupid." Amera bent forward to look into the lighted magnifying mirror. Her eye was bloodshot, veiny, and surrounded by black stuff.

"No, not you. You." Lucy pointed at me—stopping the twins in their tracks. "I'm a good person. I love the Lord, really. I go to church and I have black friends." She stood and placed her hands on my shoulders. "I even let a few black women come to my house for Bible study. Every Wednesday!"

"Lucy, she's not black. What the hell are you talking about?"

Tears fell from Lucy's eyes, leaving black streaks on her stark-white cheeks. Waterproof, my ass. "No, not her. Her boyfriend."

"No! Oh, God no. It's my bro—my ... exchange family brother, Alex." I attempted to laugh it off.

Lucy pulled back, still holding on to my shoulders. "But you said that—"

"No, no, no, Miss Lucy." I eased her hands away. "You must be confused. He's not my boyfriend."

The twins laughed.

"She would never date that loser. She has Joshua Anderson chasing her around," said Amera.

"*The* Joshua Anderson of Anderson Toyota, Jeep, Dodge," added Amelia. "Plus, we don't mix in Montgomery."

"Wait," Amera said. "Do you mix races in . . . wherever you're from?"

I shifted from one foot to the other. All three of them gawked at me, anticipating my answer like it was really important. "Right on the border of Kansas and Missouri. Most people don't realize they share Kansas City." There was a long pause as they continued rubbernecking me.

"Well?" Amelia pressed.

"Not really."

"See! She would never date a black."

Lucy took a step back. "But the way you acted . . ."

"I acted? You asked for it, lady." I cleared my throat, realizing I was raising my voice. "I mean, you were pretty unpleasant."

"Kat!" said the twins.

"She's married to our cousin's uncle or whatever." Amelia patted Lucy on the upper back.

Amera's gaze was fixated on the magnifying mirror. "She's practically family, Kat. Chill out."

"You just called her a bitch."

"Like I said—practically family." Amera backed away from the mirror and kissed Lucy on both cheeks. "If this gets infected, I'll sue." Lucy bowed her head and mouthed additional apologies. She, too, kowtowed to those ninety-pound twins—everyone did.

We walked toward the exit. "I have to go to the little girls' room. Wait here," Amelia said before jogging back to the Lancôme counter.

A few minutes later, Amelia tossed a Gus Von March bag at my chest. When I opened it, the Lily Pulitzer outfit and eighty-dollar water bra were inside.

I stopped. "I can't take this."

"Nonsense," they said.

"I can't pay you guys back." I looked at my feet as we headed to the car.

"No need, I made Lucy buy it for you with her employee discount. She really can be a bitch." Amelia climbed into the driver's seat.

Amera replied, "We barely speak to our cousin's uncle anyways. He's from our dad's white trash side."

"We play up the family angle for free makeup. And other stuff."

Throughout the ride home, I sat on the Gus Von March bag and made myself as small as humanly possible in the backseat. I peered out the window, trying to ignore the negativity spewing from the front.

I knew Amelia was driving because she'd taken the scenic route through the wealthier section of Edgewood, where single houses were nestled on acres of wooded land. Magnolia trees lined sidewalks filled with power-walking pedestrians in hot-pink jogging suits. One exceptionally skinny walker wore leggings with the exact same pattern as the Lily Pulitzer outfit in the bag beneath my butt. My hands involuntarily balled into fists. Lucy had bought the clothing. Malicious, stupid Lucy who worshipped the demons in the front seat and prejudged my kindhearted big brother at a glance. My press-on nails dug little red half-moons into my palms, and I felt the anger rise from my stomach, through my chest, and finally settle in my pursed lips.

When we pulled into my driveway, I leaped from the Bug before it came to a complete stop.

"God, Kat!" Amelia shouted.

"Yeah, don't be so eager to get away from us," said Amera. "God."

Hampton growled at the Bug's rear lights as it rolled away. When the car was no longer visible, I walked to the neighbor's garbage can, lifted the lid, and threw the Gus Von March bags inside with the rest of the trash.

YOU CAN'T HAVE IT ALL

But I wanted it all.

I wanted thrifting with my mom. I wanted to tell my dad what cars he should and should not buy. I wanted my big brother to help me find quarters. I wanted to be invited to parties where I could dress like a Barbie doll and flirt with popular boys. I wanted to ride in a car that didn't smell like diesel fuel. I wanted to feel comfortable in bathing suits and body-hugger jeans. I wanted it all, but if I had to choose, I chose Katarina.

Before Katarina, Alex and I had never gone a full day without at least one deep conversation about life, liberty, and the pursuit of popularity, but during my first week as Kat, he treated me like a pauper would treat the queen, like he was not worthy of me.

Missing Alex was a gut-wrenching consequence of the choice I'd made. I missed him so much, sometimes I couldn't concentrate.

I tried to evade my family by staying in my room during reruns of *Unsolved Mysteries*, but whenever I closed my eyes, I saw Alex climbing Colossus alone, or Mom leaving, or Dad buying another lemon of a vehicle. They were ruining everything, so I avoided all of them. I avoided talking to Dad; he never listened to my advice anyway. Stuffed earbuds in to block out Mom's morning screams and praise Jesuses; I don't know why I'd never thought of that earlier. And took showers extra early; that way Alex could have full access to our shared bathroom when he woke up.

On school days, the twins picked me up before and dropped me off after school, so I never smelled like diesel. The weekend, however, was another story. On my first Saturday morning as Katarina, I couldn't avoid my family.

Mom woke up the house at eight a.m. screaming. "Who spills coffee on their own hardwood floors? Must be crazy as hell."

"Go back to sleep, Mom." Alex stirred in his bed.

But my mother never slept past seven forty-five, and she made damn sure no one else in the house slept past eight o'clock. She'd continue her ruckus until at least one of us paid attention to her.

"How am I supposed to sleep when your daddy's walking the dog all times of night?"

Dad stayed quiet. Sometimes he elected to keep his mouth shut and disappear into his own mind. Dad was a strange man with a lot of flaws, but his feelings got hurt easier than anybody else I knew. Alex had inherited that curse. Deep emotional wounds that festered for months and years. Dad still brought up the look I gave him the one time he spanked me as a child. My attitude toward such things was I deserved the spanking—you delivered—get over it and move forward. Dad, on the other hand, couldn't let it go. Little memories built up inside and tormented him like ghosts.

"Toya!" Mom screamed. "You want to go thrifting?"

Our favorite mother-daughter pastime—thrift store hopping. While most of Edgewood's mother-daughter duos spent their Saturdays at Gus Von March, my mom and I sifted through other people's trash to find treasure. I was a brilliant thrifter if I do say so myself, but Mom sucked. She was a pipe-dream thrifter who believed every worthless tchotchke was worth a million dollars—fake fruit, ceramic white children with red lips, pretty much anything that could be purchased at the Dollar General.

I, however, could find chic treasures among all the junk. I liked the idea of clothing with a soul, so I imagined historical facts about my finds. For instance, a pink knee-length skirt may have belonged to a 1950s Southern housewife who vacuumed in high heels. Or a crisp white button-down may have been worn by Condoleezza Rice for a DC job interview; she was, after all, from

Alabama. I felt for ol' Condie. Smart, educated, powerful, but black and Republican. Black Republicans got so much crap for being black *and* Republican. Deanté called Condoleezza a sell-out, an Uncle Tom, a traitor to her race. I had never met a black Alabamian proud of her success—a shining example of black support for you.

"No, Mom. I don't feel well." I felt fine, but I didn't want to deal with thrifting with a middle-aged black woman. Too many stares to deflect. It was for her protection, really.

"Okay, but Lovelady's having an early-bird sale. Everything's fifty percent off." Any other day that would have gotten me; I was a sucker for a bargain. I had vivid dreams of a comfortable house filled with places to sit, places to eat, utensils to eat with. Every now and then, I spent the thrifting cash Dad gave me on things for the house, and then they'd always turn up missing, or broken. As a result, I focused on the decor of my bedroom, which was shabby-chic cozy.

"I'm sick, Mom." I hated lying to her.

"Please come with me. I need your help picking the good stuff." She sounded pitiful and relentless. I had to go for the jugular.

"Why don't you call Aunt Evilyn?" I shouted before burying my head in the pillow. It was one of the meanest things I could say to my guilt-ridden mother.

There was a long pause from downstairs. I imagined Mom's

head hanging low with shame. I imagined her sick with the kind of guilt moms get when they leave their kids home alone for necessary twelve-hour shifts. I imagined her shattered.

"Can I come?" Alex said from his room. Sweet Alex.

"Praise Jesus. We can stop by the pawnshop on the way." If the thrift stores were mine, pawnshops were Alex's. Alex dashed down the stairs, leaving Dad and me alone in the empty castle.

I tried hard to go back to sleep, but it was no use. I spent about an hour picking my outfit for the party later that night. I had no clue what people wore to parties. In movies, it ranged from satiny dresses to jeans. The athletic token black character would arrive late in gym spandex and tennis shoes, yelling, "Where da party at?" while the white kids laughed and high-fived their hilarious, eternally friend-zoned buddy, never once considering him or her a love interest. *The Real World* was the worst. It never failed, the black roommate was immediately categorized as BFF-material, or loud and obnoxious, or comic relief, or all of the above. Only the exceptionally beautiful black roommates were given the time of day romantically. Meanwhile, mediocre-looking white roomies were cuddled to sleep by handsome college guys with muscles. MTV casting directors made black kids want to be white without even realizing it.

In the end, I settled on an orangey floor-sweeper maxidress with little fabric rosettes lining the top. Orange didn't pop against

my white skin as it did when I was black, but the dress fit flaw-
lessly, so I went with it.

Afterward, I joined my dad on the living room pillows. I noticed
he still wore his holey sneakers.

"Did you go out?"

He looked down and chuckled. "I went for a walk," he said
before kicking off his dirty shoes in the middle of the living room
floor.

"What's with the midnight walks, Dad?" I asked. "They've
been more frequent lately."

It was as if he'd been waiting for someone, anyone, to ask how
he was doing.

"I just don't understand it." He clasped his face in his palms.
"I try, Toya. I do try. Maybe my idea of trying is different from
the next man's, but I do try." He jumped up to begin pacing the
living room. "I bought her this big house in the suburbs. I work
like a dog to pay for this thing." Hampton let out a knowing huff
of air. "Sorry, buddy. I work hard, I mean. It's never enough! This
is my first day off in two weeks. No. Seventeen days. I try every
day, and still she despises me." He sank back down on the largest
pillow across from me. "You're smarter than me. Tell me. What
am I doing so wrong?"

I didn't have enough words to explain all the things that my
father did wrong. I didn't know how to tell him that he'd crushed

my mother's dreams the day he bought the empty castle. All she really wanted was to stay at home and homeschool us, but he was too consumed with the status of Edgewood to notice such things. And not to mention his moping around the house, spilling coffee, and leaving the seat up. All in all, he was a flaming-hot mess, but I couldn't hurt him. Even if I told him, he was in no state to hear the truth about himself. I took the coward's way out.

"She'll come around, Dad."

A slight smile brightened his scruffy face. "You really think so?"

"Sure," I lied. "Oh look, *Independence Day* is on."

And then we watched one of my father's all-time favorite movies for the thousandth time. I'd always been fond of Will Smith. He didn't curse or act a fool in public. No visible gold teeth or spinner rims on his car. Just a clean-shaven regular guy who happened to be black.

"Hey, doll, your mother told me that you and Alex are having trouble." He lowered the volume of the television but didn't press mute. For Dad, that meant genuine concern. Television served as one of his only true pleasures in life, and he turned it down for *nobody*. The mute button was reserved for death or loss of limb.

"You two talk? I didn't know you and Mom did anything except fight." I immediately regretted saying it. He would mull that one over for at least a month.

He muted the TV. Uh-oh. "We've really done a bang-up job being there for the two of you, huh? We're a mess." He smiled, and I smiled right back.

"You guys do your best." I wasn't puffing smoke; I really did think that.

"So what's up with you and Alex? You're buds, always have been," he said. I watched Vivica's boobs slow-bounce away from the alien invasion. I had to give it to her, she was cute in her day. Lately, though, she pumped herself up with too much filler; cheeks, lips, butt, all of it. "All right, then, when you're ready to talk, I'll be here." He put the sound back on just in time for a Will Smith one-liner. If there was an Oscar for one-liners, Will Smith would have a mantel full.

That Saturday, TNT's *Men Who Love Movies* series showed back-to-back blockbusters. I sat there for hours soaking myself in digital testosterone side by side with my dear dad. *Independence Day* followed by *Die Hard*, followed by *Die Hard with a Vengeance* followed by *Braveheart*. Of the four, *Braveheart* was the one that made me cry like a newborn. I knew I'd get the post-cry dry headache; I couldn't help myself. The death of Mel Gibson's wife was bad enough, but the bagpipes, oh dear God, the bagpipes. I never knew bagpipes could be so depressing.

I hugged Dad and went to my room. Hugging my father was like hugging a statue; he never, and I mean never, hugged back. I could feel his love, but he had real trouble expressing it in conventional ways. His love was expressed by working overtime at the Police Dispatch to afford the empty castle, and by bringing home dollar packs of Little Debbies. I'd eaten so many Pecan Swirls by the time I started high school that the sight of them made me gag, but I could never tell Dad.

When I peered into the bathroom mirror, my eyes were bloodshot and puffy, cheeks rosy and tear streaked. As Toya, I would have looked disgusting. As Kat, I looked adorable. Just then, Mom and Alex walked in the front door, laughing and tittering at their pawnshop hop. Jealousy dashed across my chest. I was usually the one laughing and joking with Mom, not Alex. I was usually the one laughing and joking with Alex, not Mom. I felt the two of them slipping through my fingers. Jealousy was a ridiculous emotion. I had publicly disgraced my brother; so shouldn't I be happy for him? Mom and Alex joined Dad in front of the TV while I got ready for the party. After makeup, hair, and shaving, I slipped into my maxi and walked downstairs in the middle of *Rocky*.

"Ooh. You look pretty for eight o'clock at night. Where do you think you're going?" Mom tapped her fuzzy pink house shoe on the hardwood.

"I was invited to a party for the first time in my life." I figured they would have a harder time saying no if I was already dressed. "Can I go?"

Dad turned down the TV. "Why don't we just go to GC as a family? Since you're already dressed and everything." GC was the Williams family's nickname for Golden Corral, the nicest restaurant we could afford. The servers hated to see us coming, since we never left a tip. Mom had developed a strategy to avoid tipping: clean our own table, and say thanks over and over. Even when I was cute and little, I knew it never worked. Thank-yous and less crap to wipe wouldn't feed the waitresses' kids.

Headlights beamed into the living room, and the twins' horn honked twice. "My friends are here! Can I please go?"

"So you just assumed we would let you go? Or you planned to pressure us by getting dressed up and calling people to get you?" asked Mom.

She got me. "Uhhhh . . ."

The horn honked five more times. "Who are these friends anyway? If they know what's good for them, they'll stop honking that horn," said Mom.

She was right, they were foul for that. "No, Mom. They are such sweet girls. They don't mean it, I promise."

Alex let out a nose-snort snicker from the kitchen. "Alex. Get in here," Mom shrieked. Alex emerged, Debbie cake in hand. "Who are these friends picking up Toya?" she asked. He shrugged. I heard a car door open and slam. Oh God, one or both of the twins were coming to the door.

I panicked. "Please, Mom. They are going to see the house. Please, they can't see."

Dad pulled himself from the pillows. "She's right," he said. "We don't even let the pizza man past the porch. Just let her go." Dad would rather send me off to some random party than let another human being witness how empty his castle was. Not the pizza man, Jehovah's Witnesses, Girl Scouts, even the cable guy. When the cable went out once, Dad made the technician stand on the porch and yell instructions on how to fix it. We got a courtesy call the next day, telling us to call the 1-800 number if we had any more problems, and they'd walk us through it over the phone rather than roast in the Alabama sun.

"Okay," Mom said.

"Thank you!" I shot past them.

"Wait," Mom said. I had almost made it. "Alex is going with you."

I was horrified, and it must have shown, as Alex dropped his head. "I don't think she wants—"

"I couldn't care less what she wants," Mom interrupted. "You both go, or no one goes."

Hampton was barking up a storm. Amera or Amelia had to be close. "Okay, let's go." I snatched Alex's hand and drug him through the door. He was wearing a faded yellow Montgomery Biscuits baseball T-shirt with knee-length cutoff blue jeans.

Amera took one look at Alex and said, "Uh, *no.*" She turned and walked back to the car.

I followed close. "They said that I can't go without him."

"I would not be caught dead hanging out with you," Amera said, looking Alex up and down.

He stopped. "You don't even know me. And you . . ." I caught the disappointment in his voice, but I didn't dare look directly in his face. I looked at the trees, the dirt, my shoes, his shoes, her shoes (cute cobalt-blue Mary Janes), anything but his disappointed face. "How dare you let your new friend speak to me like this? If God is testing you, you're failing miserably. I don't want to go to your stupid party. I'd rather walk Hampton," he said while untying him. "Get yourself back at a reasonable time or I'm telling Mom." He disappeared into the pitch-dark woods behind our house.

"Loser," Amera called after him. "Let's go."

In the car, Amera gave Amelia the play-by-play. She called Alex every curse word known to man, but she didn't bring out the *N* word, which I took as an improvement. I wondered how far into the woods Alex had wandered. There was no path back there, and wooded vines created thick brush at the base of the longleaf pine trees. Hampton would protect him, but not in the way he needed protecting. I shouldn't have allowed him to venture into the woods alone.

"What's his deal, anyway?" I realized Amelia's question was directed to me. "Hello?"

"Oh," I replied. "I don't really know him."

"You live with him." Amera removed her seat belt to turn and glare at me. "You must know something."

I panicked. Even though I hated the twins, this was my first party ever and it felt like a massive moment in my life. I didn't want to blow it. I didn't want to come off as a concerned sister, because that wasn't my role anymore. No matter how sad it made me, I couldn't be Alex's shield. I was Katarina the powerful. Katarina the beautiful. Most important, Katarina, the girl who fit perfectly in the backseat of their Bug.

"He's a loser" came out of my mouth. And then, "He collects quarters like a child, and he wears shirts with ridiculous sayings on them."

They laughed, encouraging me to continue.

"Worst of all, he steals food from grocery stores," I added, matching their chirpy up-speak. "It's pathetic."

"That *is* pathetic." Amera rebuckled her seat belt as if satisfied with my tirade.

Somewhere deep down, I suspected that moment would come back to bite me. Hard. I shook off the dread.

Amelia changed the subject. "So, Kat, it turns out Josh

likes being dissed, because he can't keep your name out of his mouth now."

"Yeah, he told Stephen that he's only going to the party for you. . . ."

"Do guys in Ohio like punishment, too?"

"Kansas City," I said through clenched teeth.

"I thought for sure he would never speak to you again, but—"

"It made him like you even more—"

"Crazy!"

"That's what I'm saying. Crazy."

I wondered how they would ever get married. They would have to find twin brothers and live in the same house as twin sister wives to twin brother husbands and have two separate sets of twin sister-and-brother cousins. I hated them, truly, but I loved the experience. The glitz of riding in cars without parents and dressing up for parties. Boys checking me out.

"That dress washes you out a little, but you still look cute," said Amelia.

"Yeah, I'm not brave enough to wear that color. It makes me look so white." Amera glanced at her forearm. "We should go tanning tomorrow."

Tanning. Another thing I never understood about white people. They go on about how disgusting black people are and then roast like Conecuh sausages in tanning beds. I overheard Heather Hinkle and Sharon Murray in English class fighting over whose tan was the darkest. *I'm darker! No! I'm darker! You're still pasty white compared to me! Hey! I'm so dark I could pass for black! No, you couldn't! I could!* But they knew good and damn well they didn't want to pass for anything except tan white people. If they wanted to be dark so badly, why hate the people who were born that way?

We pulled up to a decent-sized Edgewood home. Edgewood was broken into sections. Ultra-snob rich Edgewood, baby-stroller-on-the-porch middle-class Edgewood, and under-the-viaduct lower-middle-class Edgewood. Even the latter homes cost nearly two hundred grand, but people dropped a cool two mil to live in the ultra-snob subdivision. This home's price tag could be four-fifty easy. We parked in the one empty place at the edge of the driveway.

"Good timing," I said.

"No. Not good timing." Amera giggled. "They always save the best space for us. Two summers ago we told everyone that we would never show up to another party if we had to walk two blocks to get to the door. . . ."

"We get what we want," Amelia completed Amera's thought.

As we climbed from the Bug, twelve white girls came barreling toward the car. Six blondes and six brunettes—the symmetry was almost comical. They bellowed compliments and praise of our outfits, hair, and shoes.

We crossed the yard into a cozy home filled with furniture. The front room had three flowered couches. Pictures lined the walls in HGTV-style haphazard synchronization. A large painted family portrait of four smiling white people and a golden retriever hung over the fireplace. Golden retrievers were sweet, but they represented the worst kind of whiteness. The kind that shouts *golly gee* when they stub a toe or *gosh darn it* when a daughter gets pregnant. Even I didn't wish to be *that* white.

"What genius decided to throw a party at this dump?" Amera asked, her face twisted with repulsion.

"I was thinking the same thing," replied Amelia. "One keg takes up half the living room."

"Whose house is this?" Amera asked no one in particular. No one answered immediately. Her question started a domino effect of partygoers asking *Whose house is this? Whose house is this? Whose house is this?* Until the dance team captain, Charlotte, timidly raised her hand and said, "It's mine, sorry."

The twins rolled their eyes and shifted attention to the party. The space was small but the energy was magnetic. Heads bobbing, kids gobbling vodka-melons—watermelon injected with vodka. No dancing, though. I had assumed no dancing at house parties; good thing, too, because I was no dancer. Southerners assumed that all black people could dance, but I busted that myth wide open. Black, white, Swedish, or otherwise, I danced like a sick chicken.

"I'm dry now," Josh whispered from behind me. What a dumb thing to whisper to a girl.

"Great for you." I didn't bother turning around. Like the twins, I couldn't understand his spiked interest. I had humiliated him. Within an hour of the swim class incident, the twins told the whole school that Josh had swim snot, yet there he was days later drooling over me. Mom says men are gluttons for punishment. They prefer women who treat them like dirt—that's why sweet loyal housewives end up with STDs. According to Mom, every sexually active person and all girls who wear bikinis have incurable STDs.

He brushed his finger down the length of my arm. "Let's talk upstairs. It's loud down here."

I followed him.

I can't say why I did it. My body led and my mind trailed behind without protest. Josh was a douche, but he still represented something that I'd wanted a piece of for so long.

No, it was deeper than wanting. I'd scrutinized him. Memorized him, like Alex would memorize a passage from *To Kill a Mockingbird* or *The Scarlet Letter*. There was a time when I could close my eyes and see which side of his head he parted his hair on. A time when I noticed fresh New Balance sneakers and new button-down shirts. When I could discern which sport he was playing depending on how his Edgewood T-shirt clung to his body. During football season, his deltoids bulged like mini steaks. When he ran track, his body leaned out. And when he swam, his entire frame formed an uppercase Y. After all those years of mental energy, my body went on autopilot and followed him up those stairs. Something inside me had to see what was waiting up there.

He ushered me into the first bedroom. The decor screamed typical teenager—unframed boy-band posters hung on all four walls; a full-sized Taylor Swift duvet covered the bed. A laptop, fancy mini-speakers, and a cell phone charging station crowded the desk.

"Taylor Swift is hot," said Josh. Taylor Swift was the golden retriever of human beings.

"What do you want, Josh?" I asked. He sat on the bed and grabbed my hand, pulling me down next to him.

"I like you. You're different." How right he was. Before I knew what was happening, he leaned in to suck on my face. My first kiss. He tasted bitter, like acid reflux and beer.

I pushed him back. "Ew! Stop with the kissing, no!" I scrubbed my lips and walked toward the door.

He grabbed my elbow. His grip was strong—and painful.

"I don't know how they do things up north, but here in Alabama, if the quarterback kisses you, you kiss him back."

"Back off! Let me go!" I screamed a Mom decibel, but the music blasted so loudly that I doubted anyone heard me.

He threw me on top of Taylor Swift, pinned my arms, and sucked my neck till it felt like he must be drawing blood. I yelled out for help, and no one came. His erection felt like a nightstick and I tried to knee him in the balls, but he was too strong; those laps in the pool paid off. "You don't embarrass me at school."

He pawed at my maxi, and that's when the breath left my chest and I couldn't find air to scream. He felt like an anvil pinning me to the mattress. My knees and elbows locked in place from what I assumed was shock. My mind, however, was as clear as the cloud-less Southern sky. How could I have been so stupid? If a guy asks you to an upstairs bedroom, he wants one thing and one thing only. I'd seen enough *Unsolved Mysteries* to know better. This was my fault.

"You don't have anything to say now, huh?" He bit down hard on my shoulder.

My body was paralyzed in place. Fear. Anger. Disappointment that I'd let myself become a statistic. My lower lip began to jump, and my eyes welled up, then overflowed.

"Jesus!" I screeched.

The door creaked open. "Whoa, whoa, whoa, sorry 'bout that, y'all," said Deanté as he started to close the door.

"Help!" I squeaked. "Help!"

Deanté reopened the door. "You attacking this chick?"

Josh slid off me, adjusting his pants. "No, I don't have to," he chortled nervously. "I have a whole gang of girls downstairs to fudge." (Only he didn't say fudge.) "She's a lying loser."

I held my elbow in the air. A bright red man-sized handprint wrapped my forearm. "He grabbed me and held me down," I said while gulping terrified breaths.

"That don't look like lovemaking to me, dude. Get out 'fore I call the cops on your ass," said Deanté.

Josh bumped Deanté's shoulder on his way out.

"Thank you so much," I gasped, nervously fixing my clothes. "I don't know what I would have done if you had not come in here. I—I—I didn't know Southern boys were like this. . . ."

Deanté stood in the doorway and crossed his arms. "You can stop talking like that, Toya. I know what's up."

BUSTED

"What?" I thought I'd heard him wrong.

"I said, drop the act. You're as much Toya as you've ever been." He grabbed a handful of tissues from the bedside table. "Are you okay?"

Dueling thoughts clouded my concentration—Deanté knew I was Toya, but I'd been attacked by Josh! I could still taste his mouth-slime in the back of my throat. It felt green and toxic, like something I wanted to vomit up but couldn't. A first kiss should be better. I'd saved it for sixteen years and it was stolen from me. A few more seconds, and Josh surely would've stolen more.

"Deanté."

He stood over me, dressed in a light-blue polo shirt and jeans, his expression wide with worry.

"Yeah?" Deanté whispered.

That's when I cracked.

He sat next to me and cradled my head between his chin and chest. He smelled freshly showered and clean, like baby-powder-scented deodorant. He gave off just the right amount of warmth to stop me from shivering, almost hot, but not quite. I stayed there until the top of his shirt was soaked dark blue with my tears.

I scrubbed my cheeks, neck, and shoulders with tissues to wipe away Josh's spit. "Thanks."

"You really need to watch the company you keep." Deanté looked sort of scared for me.

"When . . . I called Jesus, you . . . just . . . you . . . showed up," I murmured through hiccups.

"Well, I'm not Jesus, if that's what you mean." He studied his periwinkle-and-white Jordans, different color, but same design as the ones he'd humiliated me with.

"How did you know?" I said. "Do I still look black to you?"

"I know everything that goes on at that school." He sounded different. "The first day you showed up, you talked to me, remember? You talked to me in Toya's voice. Afterward, I followed you. Heard your phone call, which was hilarious, by the way." He chuckled uncomfortably and then handed me another tissue. "And heard you and Alex talking after that." His voice was as calm as a person talking about the weather. "I never knew Miss Evilyn was your aunt. That sucks. She's mean as hell."

I took a deep breath and attempted to stabilize my heartbeat. "Have you told anybody?"

"Naw, I don't spread folks' business like that," he replied. "But how did you do it?"

I told him about my prayer and Jesus's visits and Alex's exchange-student cover story. All of it. After the words flooded from my mouth, I realized just how badly I'd needed to tell someone my story, even Deanté. "You don't think I'm crazy, do you?"

"Not for the reasons that you think," he said.

"What does that mean?"

"I mean, I liked the old Toya better than this one."

"Well, without Toya, who else are you going to publicly humiliate?" Anger swelled in my belly. I glanced at a clock on the side table. It was midnight. "Oh no. I'm late! I have to get home."

"You need a ride?" Deanté asked, dangling his keys on his index finger.

"You're not going to try anything, are you?"

"No, I'll take you straight home. I promise." He held the bedroom door open for me.

Deanté's Mercedes was four blocks away. Well, his mother's Mercedes was four blocks away; she'd let him borrow it for the party. He remote-started the car long before we got inside.

My head was still spinning. But something he'd said in the bedroom didn't sit well with me. "So you said that you liked Toya better before the change. . . ."

He interrupted, "You're still Toya. Don't say it like she's dead and you're a new person."

"You should be a shrink. Not today, though. Graduate from high school first, and then college, then some more college, and then you can be a shrink. Until then, Deanté, please mind your own freaking business," I said.

"Whoa, Toya. That was the blackest I've ever heard you talk," he replied as we ducked into the car. "You want hot seats or cold seats?"

"Hot," I said, and he twisted the seat-warmer knob to high. "To be honest, I've always wondered, why do you act so black?"

"What is that supposed to mean?" He didn't seem angry—just surprised by the question.

"You know exactly what it means, Deanté," I said, but he

remained silent. "Fine, I'll elaborate. Act black as in sag your hundred-dollar jeans down around your knees. Act black as in blast hard-core rap in the Edgewood High parking lot. Act black as in hang behind the school talking Ebonic bullcrap with idiots who likely won't graduate when you're in the top tenth percentile of your class. But hey, you don't have to answer if you don't want to."

"I know that, but I'll answer," he said slowly. "We all have our place at Edgewood High. I didn't want to be an Oreo, so I chose the opposite. I went die-hard black."

"But why pretend to be something you're not?"

"I can't believe you're asking me this question with a straight face." He stared straight ahead.

"I know I'm a hypocrite, point taken, but you were crueler to me and my brother than the white people ever were. I turned my back on black for a reason, Deanté, and your group played its part. I just want to know why."

I needed to know why.

He pulled the Mercedes into an abandoned strip mall. When he placed the car in park and took his hands off the wheel, I noticed they were shaking. He clenched and unclenched his fists to steady them. "Believe it or not, I have thought about that. I'm sorry, Toya. But we all have our roles," he said, staring straight ahead at the strip mall.

"So your role is to bring down the other black people in

Edgewood to lift yourself up? To laugh at us like we're jokes? That's worse than racist, that's betrayal." I smacked the leather seat. "And it's just stupid! Ruin my life, ruin my brother's life, and you're sorry. You can keep your sorry. And you can take me home."

Deanté folded his forearms across the steering wheel and rested his forehead between his elbows. We sat in silence for an uncomfortable moment. Finally, he lifted his head and asked, "What would you have me do? Be you? Confused and lost, running from myself? No. I'm black and you are, too, whether you're wearing a white suit of armor or not. Yes, I come from a rich family. Yes, I'm in the National Honor Society. Yes, I live in a nice neighborhood. But I was born a black male in Montgomery, Alabama, which makes me a bottom-feeder just like a nigga from the hood. I accept it, and you should, too." He turned the ignition and stepped on the gas.

I wanted to slap him. I wanted to cry. I wanted to tell him he was wrong. But he was so right that it hurt. To be honest, I envied his resolve. He had in abundance what I lacked—perspective. Perspective that you are what you are. Perspective that no matter where you live or how phenomenal you are at anything, you will always be black. Perspective that you may as well accept it.

We pulled up to my driveway. "Thanks for the ride," I said as I scrambled out of the car. Deanté drove away without another word.

I stood there in the street, watching his taillights disappear. Alex's time limit had passed, and Hampton barked his family notification bark. Mom's bedroom light flickered on. Hell was about to be unleashed.

"I haven't gone in." Alex stepped out of the darkness with tiny leaves and twigs stuck in his hair. Grass and mud stains covered the knees of his jeans, and his elbow was scraped and bleeding slightly.

"My God, Alex. What happened to you?"

He looked down at himself, ready to cry. "I fell. It's dark back there."

"Why haven't you gone in? You need to clean that before it gets infected."

"I didn't go in because I didn't want our parents to know that their little girl discarded me for a bunch of *B* words. And was that Deanté? I don't even want to know how that happened. Remember when he stuck his foot out and tripped me in history? My books went everywhere, and he laughed. I lost my flash drive with all my Halo and Call of Duty codes." My brother focused on the strangest things when he got his feelings hurt.

I was done apologizing. "I'm done apologizing." I walked ahead.

"You never even started apologizing."

"That's all I've done, Alex. You're ruining this for me. If you're so jealous, just ask God to make you white, too." I'd gone too far, but I was entirely too invested to stop. "I prayed for this, and I can't even enjoy it for my loser brother sulking around all the time."

I should have just hit him. It would have hurt him a lot less if I'd just hit him.

"I'm not jealous of you, *Katarina*. I miss Toya is all. I'm glad we had this talk, though. I'd rather lose my little sister than witness her turning into this."

I looked up to see Mom standing in the doorway, her eyes filled with tears and a hint of confusion. Alex pushed past her and jogged up to his room. "I told you, Latoya Marie Williams; don't abandon your big brother."

"I get it, Mom." I went to my room, climbed in bed, and tried to cry, but couldn't. That damn *Braveheart* stole all my tears.

FORSAKEN

Sunday I slept until I heard a knock on my bedroom door. "Toya? Can I come in?" asked Mom in an uncharacteristically soft voice.

I sat up to realize it was half past two. "Yeah, come in."

Mom stepped through the door wearing a floor-length church dress and a giant sun hat that resembled a lampshade. "You missed a dynamic service this morning," she said, cradling her well-worn Study Bible like a fragile newborn. "I figured you needed some time to yourself."

I rubbed at my eye sockets. "Yeah, I did. Thanks."

She took a seat on the edge of my bed. "A lot of people gave their lives over to Christ today. A few even joined when Pastor opened the doors of the church."

"That's nice, Mom," I muttered.

"You should've seen it," she continued. "In a few more months, Pastor will have to set up chairs in the atrium. The sanctuary is running out of room."

I just nodded, picking at the loose skin surrounding my nails.

"Praise Jesus." She reached for my cheek, but I jerked away.

"I'm really not feeling well, Mom."

She nervously thumbed through the pages of her Bible. "I don't know what to do, Toya."

"Join the club," I said without looking at her.

After a fair length of silence, she left my room.

On Monday, my eyes shot open at dawn to a spastic cicada hurtling itself against my bedroom window. I let out a mini scream, not enough to alert my parents with their hallelujah chorus or to wake Alex's pitiful puppy-dog eyes—just enough to freak me out. After a dozen self-inflicted splats, the insect finally died on the outside sill, alone. The death of a cicada in Gump-town was in no way odd, but this particular bug's manner of death disturbed me. I could see it in its expressive face, its twisted body, and its serrated wings. It had taken just about all it could take. It was done with life. It wanted to die.

I gave my hair a quick brush, slipped on a pair of jeans and an Auburn University sweatshirt, and headed for the curb. The twins would despise the outfit. They prided themselves on being the most stylish crew to walk the halls of Edgewood, but I wouldn't take their crap that morning. Their usual pickup time came and went. Twice I saw the top of the Bug emerge over the hill, but they were both mirages in the form of Priuses.

"You've been stiffed, doll," said Dad.

"Shut up, man! You can ride with us, Toya. Get in now, or we'll be late," Mom said with a gentle nudge.

Wordlessly, Alex let the seat up and slid in the back as close to the opposing window as possible.

"I didn't like those gals anyway," Mom said, finishing her makeup in the shattered passenger's seat visor mirror. How she could see herself in between the cracks, I could not understand. She turned to look at us. "You guys can hang out again." She smiled wide and hopeful.

"Your lips are uneven," I told her.

She flipped the visor back down. "Man, I told you to get this mirror fixed. I go to work looking like a clown, trying to fix my makeup in this thing."

Dad whispered, "Maybe you should move back in with Evilyn. I'm sure her mirrors are perfect."

"What you say, man?"

"Nothing. Forget it," he replied softly, white-knuckling the steering wheel.

When we reached the school, no one stood at the entrance.

Alex disappeared almost immediately, and no cheerleaders jumped up and down upon my arrival. No guys gawked at my breasts. No banners or balloons or confetti or releasing of the doves. As I walked the oddly silent hallway leading to Mrs. Roseland's Alabama History, whispers arose from the shadows; the hushed *S* sounds of teenagers trying to lower their voices when they have yet to learn how. By the time I reached the first set of girls' bathrooms, the *S* sound elongated into the word *slut*. By the second set of restrooms, *Ohio slut*, and by the third set, *stupid Ohio slut*.

Stupid Ohio slut, the obvious work of the twins, seeing that they were the only idiots who thought I was from Ohio.

Mrs. Roseland's classroom door was already closed, and when my hand made contact with the doorknob, it was locked.

"No Ohio sluts allowed in Alabama History," one of the twins announced from behind me.

"I'm from freaking Kansas freaking City!"

I turned around to face Amera, who said, "Everybody knows that you're a slut."

"What are you even talking about?" I said, trying to sound more confident than I felt.

"Don't give me that crap. Josh told Stephen and Stephen told Amelia and Amelia told me what you did." She flipped her hair dismissively.

"And just what did I do?" I sounded just like my mother. Amera did a slight double take, but she was too dim-witted to put any-thing together.

"You know what you did, slut!" she screamed.

"Hey. Get to class." A substitute teacher peeked his head through a cracked classroom door. "Now, girls, go."

"See you in swim." Amera glared back at me as she rounded the corner. "Nice outfit."

I knocked on Mrs. Roseland's classroom door, and she flung it open. "Oh, sorry, sorry, sorry. I don't know how that door got locked." But I had a pretty good idea.

Walking to my desk, I noticed that the guys were no longer staring, and the girls had their pre-Katarina confidence back. Their chins held a slight lift, their hair had a noticeable bounce, and their eyes an ominous *I told you so* expression, but none were brave enough to confront me. None except the twins, so I had five peri-ods to wait before I knew what they all knew.

Between classes, I deliberately walked past Deanté and his section. They always knew the gossip; with any luck, they would let it slip.

"Eww," said Trent, one of Deanté's Jordans-wearing crew.

A girl pointed. "That's the girl. Sickening."

I looked around more keenly; it wasn't just Deanté's group. The entire student body had slowed to gawk at me.

"She was fine, too," said Trent. "Damn shame."

"What?" I said loudly, uncharacteristic of myself or Toya or Katarina or Kat—whoever the hell I was.

Deanté broke free from his posse and whispered it in my ear. "Josh is telling everybody you threw yourself at him and that you have an STD."

"Very original," I said under my breath.

"Get away from her, D. She gone give you what she got." Trent pinched his nose between his fingers.

Deanté placed his hand on my shoulder and walked back toward his crew.

"Wash that hand before you touch me, bruh," said another member of his circle.

I couldn't believe it. Well, actually, I could believe it.

Commotion arose, and students started rushing to the media center. "Fight!" someone said in the distance.

"Let's go!" someone else said.

Relieved that everyone's attention was elsewhere, I stayed planted where I stood. Then I heard it.

"Alex is kicking Josh's ass!"

It took a minute for the comment to register. But then Deanté shook my arm and said, "I think he's going to kill him, Toya."

I took off, plowing through the crowd until I saw my bloody big brother straddling Joshua Anderson's soon-to-be corpse.

"Oh my God." I walked unswervingly into the middle of the

fight. The force of Alex's whirling arms nearly knocked me back-ward. It hurt, but I didn't care. Again I stepped into the windmill and hugged him from the back until he stopped thrashing and started heaving. Josh's face and the upper part of his shirt were cov-ered in crimson. His broad shoulders looked hollow and weak. Not like a relic at all, more like the punk that he was. When he stirred, I hawked deep and spit a piece of his green toxic kiss onto his face.

The crowd expanded a bit and finally parted to welcome Officer Doug, our black off-duty cop. The band of Alex's shirt hung open, revealing a grid of scratches on his collarbone. His cheeks were bright red with fury, and his whole body still shook from adrenaline. *Braveheart* tears streamed down his face.

"All right, kid," said Officer Doug before lifting Alex into an unexpectedly kind embrace. "Let's get you cleaned up."

"Hey, Doug," some kid yelled. "You're just leaving Josh Anderson on the floor like that?"

Doug's upper lip twitched. "Call the nurse," he replied. "He'll live."

After Officer Doug carted Alex through the crowd, I ran.

Someone called after me, but I sprinted for the side door past the weed smokers and walked to Brookland Mall's Books-A-Million. I spent the remainder of the day sitting in a comfy chair and filling up on free lemon water. I flipped through magazines, but I couldn't concentrate on anything except Alex straddling Josh and pummeling the soft flesh of Josh's face without mercy. He'd never been in a fight in his life, but somehow he excelled at it. Josh, with all his swim muscles, limp on the media center floor, unable to move. Butt-kicked by my gentle brother. I smiled with pride. But then I had to wrestle back tears. I'd called him a loser and he still took up for me.

The urge to cry vanished when I thought of Josh's wickedness. If the twins were the spawn of Satan, he was Satan himself, and I'd pined over him for years. He had the nerve to suggest I'd initiated what happened up those stairs. That *I* was the slut. I felt like my skin was on fire with rage. I needed to walk.

BRYAN'S SONG

My dad needed to walk, too. Not for exercise or to get anywhere in particular, simply to rearrange his mind. I liked to think that I borrowed beautiful things from both of my parents: originality from my mom and walking from Dad.

Once, I dreamed that my father passed away. He made it to heaven for his obedience, but there were no pearly gates or golden streets, only reddish packed-dirt roads twisting themselves through plush green hills. I walked beside him for a few miles and asked him where it led.

"Nowhere," he said. He smiled his signature snaggletoothed grin. "I get to walk wherever and whenever I want. My shoes never wear down. My mouth never goes dry. No one yells at me to clean up coffee grounds. I don't have to socialize, either. Simply one foot in front of the other forever and ever and ever, amen." That night, I woke up soaked to the skin from sweat. If my dad left me, I would miss his unshaved beard and uncut hair. When I was little, I'd search for the longest strands of hair stuck to his bald spot. I loved my father, and no amount of spilled-out coffee on the foyer floor could change that.

And so I walked home from Books-A-Million—alone for the first time in my life. Through the practice fields, into the woods, past Gus Von March, around Edgewood, only to stop at the base of Colossus. It stood tall and wise, daring me to take it on. I couldn't bring myself to conquer it alone. Reaching the top would be too depressing without Alex, and since avoidance was my specialty, I took the long way around, tacking on an additional thirty minutes.

I cut through Edgewood Park. The sidewalks were teeming with moms pushing strollers, and speed walkers. On the green space, a young couple played Frisbee with their medium-sized retriever. Every time the lime-green Frisbee flew, the dog took off with pinpoint focus, and then trotted it back. The dog nearly knocked down a few toddlers on its way to retrieve the Frisbee, despite the KEEP YOUR DOG ON LEASH signs that were posted in the park.

I spotted Aunt Evilyn sitting alone on a bench, her bulgy-eyed Chihuahua, Bryan, peeking from her large purse. I should have gone home. I was white, after all, and since she wasn't immediate family, she wouldn't recognize me. But something drew me to her. I crossed the green space, stopping twice to avoid a collision with the retriever, and sat on the opposite end of Aunt Evilyn's bench.

"Excuse you, young miss," she said sweetly. "But there are three empty benches in this park. Would you be so kind as to relocate yourself to one of them?"

I laughed outright. There was something comforting about Aunt Evilyn being evil to any and everyone—it wasn't just Toya.

"Did I say something funny?" she asked, then Bryan growled and squinted at me from the purse. She caressed his protruding head. "Hush, baby. I can take care of this invasion of personal space."

"I'm on the opposite side of the bench," I said, suppressing another laugh. "How am I invading your space?"

She didn't say anything pithy in response, which was strange for Aunt Evilyn. "Lord have mercy," she said finally, staring across the park.

I followed her line of vision. A young couple released their curly blond Labradoodle and threw a yellow tennis ball. The Labradoodle shot across the green space like a bullet, but stopped cold when he spotted Aunt Evilyn. I looked from the Labradoodle to my evil aunt and back to the Labradoodle. There was history there.

She slowly lifted herself from the bench, careful not to make any sharp movements.

"What's going on here?" I asked her.

"Shut up, girl!" she snapped at me, but it was too late. Bryan locked eyes with the Labradoodle and leaped from the purse like a gazelle.

Aunt Evilyn ran after Bryan, I ran after Aunt Evilyn, and the Labradoodle stood in the center of the green space, paralyzed with fear.

"Get your goddamn dog!" Aunt Evilyn yelled for the Labradoodle's owners, who were so busy talking and chuckling that they hadn't realized their dog was about to be eaten alive, one small bite at a time.

"Oh no!" one of them bellowed. "Molly! Come here, girl!"

And then everyone was running, everyone except Molly. Bryan's hind legs straightened with every leap, covering as much ground as possible. He didn't bark. He just ran toward his target with one goal—to rid the world of this Labradoodle. He crashed into Molly and started gnawing on her front leg. Molly let out the most pitiful sound, and I zipped past Evilyn.

I dove toward Bryan. He did not appreciate my intervention,

so he turned his hatred to me. He lunged toward my arm and caught the sleeve of my sweatshirt instead of flesh. His tiny teeth were bared in rage, his eyes ready to pop out of his face.

Aunt Evilyn cupped her hands around Bryan's butt and lifted him from my sleeve. "That's it, sweet, sweet boy," she said softly, huffing for breath. "That's it." She sounded like a concerned mother kissing a boo-boo. She stuffed him back into her purse and out of sight.

Molly's family inspected her leg for marks. "That little monster bit our Molly!" said the twentysomething man in khaki cargo shorts. "What's your name, ma'am? Something has to be done about that animal." He removed his phone from his pocket.

I almost pitied him. Challenging Aunt Evilyn was a fool's errand. She was about to eat him in ways Bryan could only dream of. I waited for the downpour of insults. The attack of dignity. Anything. But nothing came from Evilyn's mouth.

Something snapped inside of me.

"Wait just one minute there," I said before swatting his phone from his hand. "There are seven signs in this park. Seven signs. Don't believe me? Let's count together." I pointed to the first sign staked near the tennis court. "One!" I yelled. Then I pointed to one nailed on the pine tree. "Two!" I yelled louder. Then the one by the walking bridge, and the pond, and the entrance, and the restrooms, and the pavilion. "Seven!"

"If anybody here needs to be reported, it's your ass for blatantly ignoring the rules of a public park. The signs are there for a reason," I said, scanning the audience for the other young couple with the Frisbee. "The same goes for you!"

They looked surprised, then offended.

I spun around like a madwoman. "That's the problem with you white people! You think you can do whatever the hell you want! You think the rules don't apply to you, but when you suffer the consequences of your *own* broken rules, it's the evil black person's fault. Bryan was in her purse, contained by his owner. He wasn't bothering anybody. But your precious Molly was *off leash*! Provoking Bryan! If anyone needs to be reported, it's you!"

Silence.

Then a handful of applause from the mothers whose children had been knocked over by the Frisbee-retrieving retriever.

"Woo!" one of the young white mothers said. "Damn right! That dog nearly gave my Kenny a concussion."

She pointed at the Frisbee family, and they slowly backed away and disappeared.

Molly's owners stood still, shocked by my outburst. Molly whimpered as if encouraging her owners to tuck tail and leave. Then the man snapped Molly's leash on and picked up his phone.

"I'll drop it this time," he said pompously, before walking away. "You're just as white as I am, you know," he added.

My blond hair got caught in a breeze and swung into my line of sight. I ran home, leaving Aunt Evilyn standing in the middle of Edgewood Park.

ABSENT

"Mom, can I stay home?"

"Of course. I knew you weren't feeling well when you missed revival last night. Rest well, baby. The rest of y'all, *come on*," screeched Mom.

Mom and Dad weren't angry about the fight. They'd always told us to take up for one another, and since Alex was fighting for Toya, no punishment necessary.

At school, on the other hand, Alex got ISS (in-school suspension) for two weeks. Alex and I had always wanted ISS. It seemed easier than regular school. No forced social interaction, no reading aloud, no cafeteria; just cubicles filled with books. That's not punishment, that's paradise. I was happy for Alex. He deserved it.

While I was thankful for the day off, I couldn't shut down my mind. Deanté, Alex, Mom, Dad, Aunt Evilyn, the twins, Josh—even *Braveheart* made its way into my brain. The bagpipes, oh dear God, the bagpipes. Mostly, I kicked myself for calling my brother a loser to his face. I knew that I needed to stop talking, but my woman motor took over.

My woman motor was usually fueled by estrogen and premenstrual syndrome, but between Deanté's lecture and Josh's attack, I was an atomic warhead of built-up anger, disappointment, frustration, anxiety, and confusion. Typically, I could aim it away from my brother, but Alex just happened to be there when I exploded. It felt like a release, but this time regret was left in its wake—that's how the woman motor works.

I turned on the television for distraction, and it just made me angrier. My favorite channels were littered with black women fighting like cats on reality shows, or half-naked singers bouncing their behinds inches from the camera lens. I tried watching the morning news, then during Montgomery's Most Wanted segment, there were not one but two Latoyas listed. One for tax evasion and the other for possession of a forged instrument, whatever that means. After that, I flipped the TV off and threw the remote.

The only decent thing about PMS was the hibernation sleep:

ten, twelve hours easy. I squeezed myself into a tight fetal ball and fell asleep quickly.

I flew out of my bedroom window. When I looked to my left, my arm was covered in translucent feathers, and extra cartilage helped me climb toward the clouds. I knew it was a dream and I didn't care one bit; flying was just as exceptional as it looked. Gazelles, deer, bears, and lions grazed together in my backyard. No species trying to eat the other, only harmony. The absurdity of prey and predator made me laugh out loud as I climbed upward. The clouds wet my skin; black skin, Toya's skin. I knew that the wetness of the clouds would frizz my hair, so I looked for a place to land and dove toward a grassy stretch of green. My feet touched the earth, and then I planted myself firmly at the fifty yard line of Edgewood High School's freshly mowed practice field.

"Haven't heard from you in a while." Jesus motioned me to sit next to him on the bleachers.

My wings shrank into regular arms as I walked toward him. Taking my seat, I realized that I hadn't called on Jesus as much as I had when I was Toya. "Yeah, I'm sorry."

"Your mother is right, you know." He didn't elaborate, because I knew he was talking about Alex—and he knew that I knew. "So, are you enjoying life as Katarina?"

"It's fine," I said. "Actually, that's not entirely true. It's much more complicated than that."

"Complicated?" he asked.

"Just . . . being white is not as easy as I expected." I didn't want to disappoint him, but I couldn't bring myself to lie.

"Well, nothing ever is."

"Why, though? I mean, why grant me a wish, then set me up to be assaulted and called names?" I felt the frustration rising from deep inside. Though it was a dream, I had complete control over myself. I knew exactly what I was saying and doing.

He knuckled my tear away from my cheek before I realized it was there. "You begged me. You cried, screamed, yelled, and cursed for years, Latoya. I said no well over a thousand times, and then, we gave you what you asked for. Exactly what you asked for. Unfortunately, sometimes what we want is not necessarily what we need."

"Can you stop playing games, and just tell me what I should do?" I said louder than I'd intended.

"I cannot."

I stood to my feet. "Fine. Well, I want to be Brazilian tomorrow."

"That's not a race, it's a nationality."

"Whatever!" I stood over him. "That's what I want to be next. Can you do it?"

He shook his head no.

"What?" I asked in disbelief.

He shook his head again, and his pewter eyes peered so deeply into mine that my head began to ache. "Wake up."

When I opened my eyes, my nightshirt clung to my skin like a Band-Aid. The sweat made the green squiggly veins in my forearm glisten in the newly risen sun.

"White," I said to myself. "Thanks for nothing."

The clock read 5:07 a.m.—way too early to start getting ready for school, but I couldn't go back to sleep. I pulled the covers over my chin and tightened myself in like a caterpillar. The dream haunted me. In all our interactions, Jesus never seemed disappointed in me, but when he'd looked into my eyes, I felt his anxiety. His desperation for me to understand something I couldn't grab ahold of.

I reflected on my prayer—*anything but black, Lord, anything but black.* It was the most sincere prayer I'd ever prayed. Before that night, faith felt like an ethereal, unattainable thing. I loved the Lord, but I hadn't truly believed that the faith of a mustard seed could move mountains. Then something powerful happened. After I buffed the dent from Deanté's Jordans, a switch flipped inside me from questioner to believer. And I'd never been so sure of anything in my life: White would be better.

Now, I wasn't so sure.

I quietly entered the bathroom and turned on the computer to search the Internet for evidence of Jesus answering unanswerable prayers. After nearly fifteen minutes, the frustratingly slow hourglass converted into a workable arrow, and I Wikipediaed "Miracles of Jesus." His marvels were neatly categorized into a gallery. The cures were first, including things like healing the blind, cleansing lepers, and fertilizing barren women. Then came exorcisms, followed by resurrections, both fairly self-explanatory. The last set of miracles was the most impressive—control over nature.

Walking on water was my Sunday school teacher's favorite phenomenon, so I knew a fair amount about that one, but there was one that hadn't been adequately explained to me—transfiguration. After a full thirty minutes of research, I barely understood it myself. My interpretation was: Jesus wanted his disciples to realize that he wasn't just a prophet, he was the full-on Messiah. So he took them up a Colossus-style hill and transformed into something undeniably awesome. That way they would know, once and for all, that he was the Son of God. That was cool and all, but it wasn't the part that got my attention.

While Jesus was up there, he brought two of his dead buddies along—Moses and Elijah. Moses was the first of God's prophets, and Elijah was a great prophet, too. Both Moses and Elijah performed mighty works back in the Old Testament days, and they'd both experienced rejection from their own people. That was the connection. I wasn't stupid enough to believe that I was as awesome as Moses or as fabulous as Elijah. From my brief research, I surmised that Jesus had a soft spot for the rejected.

I clapped my hands and shut off the computer.

"Man! Did you pay the water bill?" Mom yelled from downstairs. When Dad didn't answer, I knew that he hadn't. Mom's intentionally heavy steps echoed from one bathroom to the next, and finally up the stairs toward my room.

"Toya," she said, banging on my door like the police. "Let me in, I need to tape your commode. Your daddy's already dropped loads in two of the downstairs bathrooms, so y'all have to squeeze your butts closed till you get to school. I can't take this shit!" She paused. Wait for it . . . wait for it . . . "Lord forgive me." Mom rarely used curse words that weren't in the Bible; when she did, she'd spend ten or so minutes asking for God's forgiveness. "Lord, Lord, Lord, please forgive me." As she walked away begging for God's clemency, I heard Alex urinating into our unflushable upstairs toilet.

While I was certain Mom would let me take another day off, the pong of morning urine and downstairs double doo-doo began permeating my muggy bedroom. Besides, Alex elected to take the day off from ISS, and I didn't want to deal with his awkward energy. I threw on a knee-length blue jean dress with two oversized pockets large enough to hold on to my hands if they began shaking, when I heard a knock coming from the bathroom.

"Toya?" Alex said softly.

"I'm sorry," I answered. "Oh, and thanks for the whole Josh thing. I was so proud of you. You turned him into a big pile of pitiful. I couldn't believe—"

"Look at this on your way to school," he interrupted before sliding a booklet under the door. "It's for Roseland's pop quiz." I heard his bedroom door closing.

"Alex?"

The door stopped before meeting its latch. "What?" he asked.

"Has anyone said anything to you about Toya?" I asked. "I know it's a long shot, but I was just wondering if someone, I don't know, misses her."

"They don't matter," he sighed. "Why don't you get that?"

"Does that mean no one asked or—"

"No," he snapped. "No one." His door slammed.

Skimming through the booklet, I saw he'd highlighted the especially important sections—Alabama's state bird, tree, and flower. The yellowhammer, Southern longleaf pine, and camellia, respectively. A single tear fell from my right eye.

In the Fiat, I sprawled across the entire backseat.

"You okay?" Mom asked. "You didn't eat any of the black-eyed's in the refrigerator, did you? I think they went bad."

I ignored the question and squeezed myself into a tight backseat ball.

"I ate the whole pot last night, and I feel just fine," Dad replied.

"You didn't see the green film floating on the top? That was mold. What you trying to do, man, kill yourself?"

"Tasted good to me. I thought it was okra." Dad shrugged. "Humph, maybe that's why I had to go twice this morning."

I plugged my ears, but I could still make out the *damn fools*, and *shut up, woman*s all the way to school. When the car slowed, I unblocked my ears.

"Okra is more Kermit green; mold is a brownish green. You been living in Alabama almost fifty years, and you don't know the difference between mold and okra? You crazy, man."

"You know that I'm color-blind, you mean ole mule!" Dad missed a gear and stalled out.

"Dad!" I yelled, almost involuntarily. "Why do you always have to stall out at the entrance of school? Everybody's looking."

He readjusted the stick shift toward neutral. "I'm sorry, sweetheart. I'll try to—"

"He just can't drive worth a damn."

"Mom!" I shouted. "Stop treating Dad like shit all the time! Can't you see he's trying?"

Dad spun his head toward me, completely shocked. "Latoya, don't you ever—"

Mom held her hand in the air, shutting him up. "Lord forgive her," she said to the ceiling of the Fiat. "You can take a day if you—"

"No," I interrupted. "I can do this."

GRIDIRON

Edgewood prided itself on Josh, the most popular, handsome, talented, and kind football player in school. He volunteered at the food pantry, was elected Student Government Association treasurer, and dominated not only football but track and field and swim, too.

On the surface, he was impeccable. Edgewood's very own Prince Charming. The perfect height, the perfect build, and Lord knows, the perfect color for Edgewood. I'd imagined us married, sharing a last name, a home, and the responsibilities of his father's dealership. Sharing children with lightly sun-kissed skin and loose curls. I'd scribbled his name on the next-to-last page of all my notebooks, filling the empty white spaces with hearts and arrows and fat-legged cupids. I'm sure every other girl at Edgewood

High School had done the same. My pulse raced when he asked me to pass the honey mustard. His lowly condiment request possessed the power to improve my day, and that's too much power for anyone, especially Josh.

Meanwhile, I'd reserved a special place in hell for Deanté. Deanté—the opposite of everything I'd held dear. The predetermined villain of my story. Granted, Deanté earned much of my disdain, but I was in no way faultless. Honestly, I knew that I was no better than Lucy and the rest of the Gus Von Marchers. I'd prejudged him in the same way they'd prejudged my big brother. Deanté was right. No matter what he did, or said, or wore, he was still black. And in Montgomery, Alabama, black is a threat, even to other black people.

I hated Edgewood High School. I hated Lucy, I hated the twins, I hated my own self, but most of all, I hated Josh. The blood in my veins began to heat up at the hopelessness of it all. There was no remedy, only a slew of unsuspecting girls to be led into that upstairs bedroom, and not nearly enough Deantés to save them.

I gulped, remembering the pea-sized chunk of saliva he'd lodged into the back of my throat. The memory of it wouldn't go down, and I wasn't sure if it ever would. I still tasted his sour, aggressive tongue; its texture was coarse and harsh like a Brillo Pad extracting baked-on grease from a dish.

I stood in the frenzy of changing classes, but I heard nothing. The noisy, chaotic hallways of Edgewood High went completely quiet around me. A freshman girl dropped a handful of papers, the Jordans pointed and laughed, Mrs. Roseland waved, but I was no longer there. It was as if I'd developed a force field that filtered out everything except Josh Anderson. My own world of Josh where all I could see was his smirk. All I could smell was his funk. And all I could feel was his erection forcing its way into places I didn't want it to be. I felt trapped by him, cornered by his repulsive existence.

I needed to break free from the bubble of Josh, and I knew the only way to do that would be to expose him. But exposing him seemed like an insurmountable task. He was their golden boy, their . . .

"Fuck it," I said.

I shouldered my way through the hallway toward the no-pay pay phone. If I didn't find a way, I might never rid myself of the lump in my throat. The only idea I could come up with was to call and report Josh to the principal's office. The media center was empty with the exception of the helper, who was fast asleep as usual, so I called the principal's office, hoping they did not have caller ID.

"Edgewood High School. May I help you?" said Ms. Wade, the Gatekeeper. To my surprise, she had a pleasant phone voice. I guessed it was a put-on for parents or upper-level management, but I had a straight-shot view of her through the library window—lo and behold, she was flipping a damn catalog.

"I would like to report an attempted rape." When she lowered her catalog, I knew I had her. Those eyes grew so large I could see her pupils clearly through three sets of thick glass.

"Hold, please." She rose from her beloved swivel chair and banged on Principal Smith's office door. She burst through, disappearing into his office and reemerging seconds later. "The principal is in a meeting," she said as Principal Smith peeked at her through his cracked door.

No offer to take a message, just lies. Big white lies of Edgewood High.

A flicker of anger sprinted up the center of my spine. "Look, lady. If you don't transfer me to the principal, I'll call Birmingham news and report you for institutional neglect." Birmingham was the most progressive city in Alabama.

She stuttered something unintelligible, eyeballed the principal, and said, "You're calling *Birmingham* news, you say?" They exchanged hectic sign language. I watched her lower the phone. At first, I thought she was hanging up, but after a click, I realized she'd placed me on speakerphone.

"Yes, Birmingham," I said, sensing their fear. "I know Edgewood has Montgomery media in their deep pockets, but Birmingham has the Southern Education Desk at their NPR station."

After a whispered exchange with his Gatekeeper, Principal Smith quickly shut his office door.

"I'm going to transfer you to the principal's line."

I'll be doggoned, so that's how you get transferred back there. "Principal Smith speaking," said the stately gentleman's Atticus Finch voice, which I'd only ever heard over the intercom.

"Yes, I need to report an assault. It happened at a party Saturday night, and it would have gone further if someone hadn't walked in on us," I said, barely pausing to breathe. "He held me down. I'm pretty sure I still have his handprint on my forearm. He was so strong. Too strong for me to handle, and I think he may try this type of thing again." Something occurred to me that I hadn't thought of. "I'll bet he's done something like this before."

"Does this boy attend Edgewood High School?" His voice simmered like a teakettle about to squeal.

"He does," I said, trying not to break down, but the thought of Josh's hands wrapping around my forearms, his breath on my neck, and his sour spit in my throat made me want to rip the phone from the wall and throw it through the glass.

"I need a name."

167

"His name is Josh Ander—"

"Of Anderson Toyota, Jeep, Dodge?" he asked before a panicky chuckle. "Our quarterback? Oh, no, ma'am, I assure you he's not that type of boy."

"Not that type of boy?" I shot from the stool with such force that I could barely stay on my feet. "He nearly fractured my arm, dumbass!"

"Well, there's no need to use that type of language. What's your name, young lady?"

"Why do you need my name? I gave you the name of the bastard who tried to—"

He interrupted, "If you don't give me a name, there's nothing I, or anyone, can do."

"I will not give my name," I said firmly before hanging up in his face.

The principal stormed from his office, flailed his arms back and forth, and went back to his desk. I watched in utter disbelief as the Gatekeeper recrossed her legs, picked up the catalog, and resumed her flipping. I gave them a few moments to reconsider. Then I gave myself a few more moments to understand: understand that being a girl comes with much responsibility. Not just a white or black girl, or a hot or not-hot girl, but any type of girl. The responsibility to fiercely protect our bodies from monsters who think they can take what they want and get away with it. And then, as final adornment, they spread the rumor that *we* initiated it, effectively checking the slut box for us.

There was no textbook or class period dedicated to living with the burden of being born with a vagina. No dummy's guide to avoiding bellicose penises attached to entitled boys with Edgewood clout. Only trial and error, and hopefully true friends to confide in. When I thought about it, the only true female friend I had in the world was my mother.

My mother could never know I'd been attacked, because I didn't want to be lumped into what she referred to as the "running-in-the-woods girls." Whenever a white girl went missing on *Unsolved Mysteries*, my mother would say, "I bet she was running in the woods by herself in butt-out shorts." Usually, Mom was right. Not that she blamed them for their *Unsolved Mysteries*—worthy predicaments, but her tone suggested that some responsibility fell on the victim. I wanted my mother to think I was smarter than that, even if I wasn't. Besides, Lord knows I didn't want to be responsible for her heart attack, or the prison sentence she would receive from cutting off the quarterback's wiener. So I resigned myself to finding another way.

By lunchtime, my head pounded. Though I'd chosen the table farthest from the Chosen Table, the whisper clusters throughout the lunchroom created one giant whisper-holler, defeating the purpose of whispering altogether. Most of the chatter was about Josh's fat lip and black eye. But some were talking about me.

Trolling the cafeteria, I saw the black people arrive. If I hadn't been watching, I would have heard them, as they were by far the loudest group in the lunchroom. One of Deanté's friends, Andre, pointed directly at me and said something into his girlfriend Tiffany's ear. I picked up my plastic spork and began poking my wayward green peas, but that didn't stop them from snaking their way to my table.

"So what you got?" Andre and Tiffany slid into the empty seats across from me. "I Googled some pics of STDs, and that shit is crazy. You got the one that looks like yellow broccoli?" he asked. Tiffany was stifling a laugh. I sank my head forward and tried to ignore them. "Hey! Over here, y'all." He waved four more of his friends, including Deanté, toward my table. "I'm just asking this chick what she got going on in her *draws*."

"Andre, chill with that, bruh," said Deanté. I looked up and locked eyes with him. I never thought I'd see the day, Deanté standing up for someone his friends were picking on.

"D, what's the matter with you? You been talking like a white boy and acting like a bitch lately," said Andre.

"Whatever, dude. Just chill. She obviously doesn't want to be bothered."

"Dude?" Andre seemed shocked by the word. "You saying *dude* now?" When Deanté didn't reply, Andre sucked his teeth. "Come on, y'all. Let's go. Looks like we done lost Deanté to the white folks," he said, leaving Deanté standing there.

He looked at the seat that Andre had vacated. "Can I?"

AN UNEXPECTED JOURNEY

"Don't let them get to you," Deanté said.

"That's funny, I was going to say the same thing to you. What just happened?" I asked.

"They say I've been acting white." He shrugged. "I don't know."

"I must say, your English has improved."

"I know how to speak." He looked around to make sure no one was listening. "Toya," he whispered. "I thought about what you said. You shamed me into subject-verb agreement." He tapped his fingers on the table. I noticed that his nails were clean and cut down evenly—rare for a Southern boy.

"But what about your precious place in Edgewood High School society? Your role, as you called it." He began poking one of my green beans with the unused plastic knife. He wouldn't look at my face, but I could tell that he was listening intently. Watching my mom demand immediate action from my dad, with no result, helped me realize that men were listening, they just needed extra time to absorb before they implemented a woman's words. Maybe it's pride or stupidity, who knows, but no man will jump when a woman says jump.

"Edgewood High will be just fine. Hopefully, I'll have you to hang out with. Not you like this but when you turn back, I mean. When are you planning on doing that anyway?" he asked a bit too eagerly.

"Omigosh. I think this is the oddest couple I've ever seen in my life. . . ."

The twins switched past our table so closely that I could smell their Chanel.

"The oddest . . ."

"By far . . ."

"Oops!" Amera dropped her plastic cup of ketchup onto my ballet flats.

"Oops!" Amelia followed suit with some mustard.

They laughed as they walked away. "Now your shoes look as disgusting as your vag."

"Good one, Amera!"

"Thanks, Amelia." They high-fived and exited the cafeteria.

Everyone was watching, some sniggering and some pitying, but

I couldn't let them see me break. I grabbed my book bag and ran toward the courtyard.

"Wait up!" Deanté shouted after me.

The courtyard was empty. I sat on the concrete bench, surrounded by bright blue hydrangea bouquets as big as my head.

When the door scraped open, I didn't look up to see who it was. "Please, leave me alone," I said.

"It's just me. Can I stay?"

Deanté snipped a hydrangea and held it beneath my chin. I smiled despite myself. "You can get in trouble for doing that."

"I don't really care." He smiled. I had never noticed the dimple on his left cheek. I wanted to stick my pinkie in it.

"Yeah, sit," I said. He scooched in close enough to raise the tiny hairs on my forearm. He smelled clean like laundry detergent. Not the cheap kind, though; probably Tide and Downy—the rich-people combo.

"White isn't all it's cracked up to be, huh?"

I shook my head.

"How about you just change back to the real Toya like I said? I'm sure Alex would appreciate it. Remember him? Just looking at him now makes me depressed."

I couldn't talk about Alex. "You want to hang with me, why?" I looked down at my formerly white shoes, splattered with yellow and red.

174

"I told you I liked you as Toya." He uncrossed his legs and shuffled his feet in the grass. I noticed that he wore beige boots instead of sneakers and that made me glad, because I hated the sight of those Jordans. They reminded me of the Deanté who made me bow down at his feet. I inched away, attempting to gain a bit of space between us.

"You sure had a horrible way of showing it." I folded into myself, slumping until my elbows met my thighs.

He started a few sentences, but gave up after a couple of tries. He dropped his head back, clearly frustrated with himself. "I can't take back the messed-up things I've done. I don't know, Toya. I just want you to come back so I can really make it up to you." He took my hand.

But I snatched it away. "You all think that you can just treat girls however the hell you want, and then we'll fall to pieces when you soften your voices and snuggle up close smelling like really good detergent. Well, that's not how it works, Deanté."

"Wait a minute," he said. "Who is 'you all'?"

"I don't know, all of you," I said, fighting the urge to sob. "Boys!"

He shifted nearer, effectively closing the small gap I'd created. "What's going on?"

"I wanted the boys to look my way, and God gave it to me." I rubbed my forearms to keep the goose pimples at bay. "As a black girl, I was invisible. I know that sounds like a Southern cliché, but it's the God's honest truth. I could've walked up and down the hallways of Edgewood High School in a pink tutu and sequin bra, and no one, besides your group, would've paid me any mind."

Deanté opened his mouth to speak but quickly changed his mind.

"I know you're sorry, I can feel that, it's just the truth. The only popular black kids at Edgewood are exceptional at sports, or singing, or dancing. If you don't have something extra special, you're nothing. It's not like that for the white ones. You don't need a superpower to stand out. Take Amera and Amelia . . ."

"Oh God, can we not—"

"Hear me out, Deanté," I interrupted. "They're the most popular girls in the sophomore class, maybe the entire school. Their parking space is reserved at parties, and they've split the Homecoming crown two years in a row. People bow when they walk down the hallways, for goodness' sake. What have they done to deserve that coveted tip of the pyramid? Nothing. Edgewood requires nothing of them. The only default requirement is their whiteness."

Deanté lifted his hand to the small of my back, and for whatever reason, I let him. "Toya," he said. "If you listen to them, I mean really listen beyond their nastiness, they're miserable." His thumb rubbed tiny circles on my back. "They hate themselves just as much as the rest of us hate them. It's just harder to see underneath that shiny crown."

He was right. Why else would they torture themselves with starvation? And go out of their way to hurt people who didn't deserve to be hurt? The twins were fools dropping condiments on shoes and making fun of kids with Down syndrome. They possessed power because we gave them power, not because they were worthy of it. The realization sent shock waves through me, lifting some of the burden that had been weighing me down.

Deanté drew his hand away from my lower back. "What?"

I lifted my hand to his chin, and the invisible stubble tickled the tips of my fingers. "Actually, you're pretty wise." When his cheek began to twitch, I withdrew my hand and immediately regretted touching his face.

We sat until he began a breathy whistle to fill the silence.

"I told on Josh, and the principal didn't do anything about it," I blurted.

"You know better than to tell the principal. Next fall's football season is too promising," Deanté said matter-of-factly, which made it worse. "He's assaulted other girls, and no one's done anything about it."

My God.

"Two that I know of," he added.

"I'm . . ." I needed a moment to take it all in. I wanted to scream.

I doubled over and cradled my face. My nose was so close to my shoe that the vinegar in the ketchup made my stomach turn.

"Hey, I'm sorry to lay this on you." He touched my shoulder. "I shouldn't have . . ." He trailed off.

I kept my gaze away from him. "How do you know all this?"

"Like I said, nothing happens at this school that I don't know about. That's how I knew where you were at the party." He commenced shuffling his boots again.

My heart beat so hard that I could hear it. "You saved me . . . on purpose?" He twirled the hydrangea between his index and middle fingers. His eyelashes were shiny black and long like a girl's. His skin smooth and chocolaty. Little black hairs stuck straight out of his head; too short to curl, but I could tell that they wanted to. I'd never noticed those things before. He bit his lip, hard. "Deanté. Look at me." He looked into my eyes.

"You know, you still have the same eyes as Toya. Different. But the same."

"Thank you for saving me."

"I wanted to save the others, but I was too late," he said. "I should've beat his ass back then. Alex sure let him have it, though, didn't he?" A little while passed before either of us spoke again. My mind was wild with gratefulness toward Deanté, regret for the other girls, anger toward Josh, frustration with myself for walking up the godforsaken stairs. I couldn't fix my thoughts on any one thing.

"Hey," he said in a hushed voice, and then he nudged me. "I'd like it if you'd hurry up and change back." The dimple showed up again, giving me something to focus on.

I reached toward his face to stick my finger in it when the weed-smoking crew burst through the courtyard doors.

My pinkie was less than an inch from his cheek when he jumped from the bench and stuffed his hands in his pockets. Standing in front of me, he asked, "You busy Saturday?"

"No, why?"

He kicked at a wobbly rock. "My mom says I can have her car for a few hours. I want to show you something."

"What?"

He held the hydrangea in front of me and peered keenly into my eyes. "Why it's not so bad to be black."

I snatched the flower and rolled my eyes instinctively, assuming he was kidding, but he continued to stare until I spoke. "How do you plan—?"

"Guys! Want to spark up with us?" interrupted one of the stoner kids.

"No!" Deanté and I said in unison.

"Okay," I replied to Deanté. I'd known him for years but never noticed that dimple.

"Good, then. I should get going." He tripped on his way to the door. And I laughed.

That dimple haunted me throughout Barnhouse's biology. How could I miss something so precious? When the ocean whooshed, I realized that I had doodled Deanté's name onto my notebook twelve and a half times.

I JUST DON'T KNOW ANYMORE

"Toya, you riding with us?" Mom hollered.

"Yes," I replied.

"Well, come on!"

Alex already sat in the backseat; same ol' courteous big brother, he'd left the seat up for me to climb in beside him. His upper body was even more hunched than the last time I'd ridden with him. He'd walked Hampton through the woodsy backyard the night before, and there were a few leaves in his unbrushed hair. I lifted my hand, reflexively, to pick them out.

He caught sight of my approach and recoiled. "Please don't touch me," he said softly.

"You have a few leaves in your hair," I said, fighting the overwhelming sensation to blubber.

Mom looked back at us. "I'll get them." She forced a smile and proceeded to remove the leaves.

"I appreciate that, Mom," he said before quietly handing me another booklet. This one had my name printed on the front instead of his. "Barnhouse's cell cycle project is due today. It's half your overall grade."

I knew he was still mad at me. The mean crease between his eyes gave him away. For Alex, doing my homework was more pity than forgiveness. He was naturally brilliant, and I'd never been a good student as Toya, but as Katarina, I was atrocious. I couldn't find the words. *Thank you* really wasn't enough, and *I'm sorry* felt misplaced. I could've told him how much I loved him, but I didn't want him to think I was saying it just because he'd done my homework for me.

Mom broke the silence. "That's really sweet, Alex. Isn't that sweet, Latoya?" she said.

I nodded.

The rest of the ride was silent except for the *clankity-clank* of the engine. Riding to and from school in the squeaky-clean Bug had spoiled me for the Fiat. I'd surely hated the Fiat before, but by now, I downright loathed it.

To distract myself from the jerky ride, I compiled a mental list of the people I needed to make amends with; incidentally, three of them were riding in the car with me. My mother kept glancing in the backseat; in her way, nudging the kinks out of Alex's and my relationship. Dad repeatedly shot looks into the rearview mirror until he and I locked eyes. In those seconds, his eyes were glassy, and more expressive than I'd ever seen them—pleading with me. He looked away and didn't look again.

Once we hit school grounds, I leaned close to Alex. "I'm sorry."

"It's cool. You have to get out first." I'd lost him and I knew it. I caught sight of a white letter sticking out of his pullover's pocket, and my stomach gurgled. He still hadn't told me what they were about, and he probably never would.

For Alex, apathy meant more than anger or sadness or depression. It meant *that's it, it's over, I'm done.* Scary thought, because if I didn't have Alex, who did I have?

Deanté was perched against the brick wall near the school's entrance. He wore a white T-shirt, not the dingy kind with armpit stains, but the thick cotton kind that costs thirty dollars at Gus Von March. When I got closer, I saw the blue polo man embroidered near his heart—make that fifty dollars. His jeans were intentionally faded in all the appropriate places to make them designer, and his sneakers were as white as his T-shirt. Deanté had been voted Best Dressed two years in a row, but I'd never really looked at him, especially since he used to terrify me.

I looked around for Alex and caught the curve of his backpack disappearing around the corner. I'd found him that backpack. Mom and I were at Mission Possible, searching through tiny porcelain mammies, and little white Pilgrim salt and pepper shakers, when I saw it buried underneath a half-bald Chucky doll. Later, I thanked my lucky stars for that Chucky doll—surely the thrifters who came before were too terrified to lift it and find the treasure that lay beneath. The backpack was brown leather with sturdy silver buckles and red dirt caked in the bottom right corner. It looked like it'd been through hell, which only made it look cooler. The inner label read MULHOLLAND DEERSKIN RUCKSACK, and it sold for over a thousand dollars on eBay—twelve dollars at Mission Possible. I would've kept it for myself, but when we got home, Alex locked eyes on it and fell hard and fast for the thing. If love at first sight existed, I'd witnessed it then and there. It was his.

"Hey," Deanté said, breaking my trance.

"Oh, sorry. Hey."

He followed my gaze. "Alex?"

I nodded.

"He'll come around." He held the door open for me to walk through. "Well, if you're not excited about tomorrow, Miss Lady, you should be. I've got it all planned out."

"Where are we going anyway?" I replied, grateful for the change of subject.

"It's a surprise. You like surprises, right? 'Cause I don't want to freak you out. I mean, I thought about it last night and I know some people really hate them. Do you? Hate surprises?" He barely took a breath.

"You just said the word 'surprise' like twelve times in one sentence." I smiled a bit. "And no, I don't care for surprises. Just tell me."

"'Ey, yo, D!" shouted Andre.

"Just keep walking," said Deanté.

I couldn't help but think of the time Deanté called after Alex and me, and Alex told me to keep walking away from him. My big brother had protected me from the guy who was protecting me now. The thought took hold of my muscles, and I nearly fell over.

"Why are you stopping? He's just gonna give us crap," said Deanté.

I stood as straight as possible and turned to face Andre head on. "There will always be crap. Might as well face it," I said, surprising myself with the firm undertone in my voice.

Andre started, "So you and the white girl? That's disgusti—"

"Can I ask you a question?" I interjected.

He snickered and took a slight step back. "Go 'head, as long as you don't touch me."

"I want you to answer honestly. No bullshit." Like my mother,

I hated curse words. I sounded ridiculous saying them out loud, but Andre deserved no less than the real thing.

"Yeah, aight." He folded his arms and lifted his chin.

"Are you a man or a little boy?" I asked, taking a page directly out of my mother's belittle-the-opposite-sex playbook.

He let out uncomfortable laughter, the kind that you release when you trip over an invisible pothole and your crush is watching. "What kind of question is that? You can't expect me to—"

"Actually, I do expect you to answer, because you said you would." I inched closer to him, refusing his intimidation. "Are you a man, or are you a little boy?"

"D, get your girl," he said to Deanté, massaging his fists.

"Toy . . . uh . . . Kat. Come on." Deanté eased his finger back into the crook of my elbow.

I noticed a small crowd growing as I slipped my arm from Deanté's grasp. "No, I'm not afraid of him," I said, actively quieting my knocking knees.

Andre stood squarer and grabbed hold of his crotch. "I'm a man, can't you tell?" he chuckled, then looked around to see no one joining in his laughter.

"What type of man listens to high school gossip and openly teases a girl about it?" I asked, my nose inches from his.

He said nothing.

"What type of man ostracizes his best friend for speaking correct English?"

He said nothing.

"I'll tell you what type of man: none!" I said the last word with a piercing screech. When I poked his chest with my index finger, the crowd let out a collective breath followed by hectic chatter. "Only little boys do that." On that note, I walked away.

I never turned back to see if he was still standing there, but I guessed he was. There was no way to tell if my words made a difference, but they'd shaken him, and that was enough for me.

I replayed the Andre incident over and over that day. The initial gratification of crushing such a puffed-up human being so easily was blissful, but it didn't last. I never wanted to inherit any semblance of my mother's talent for demeaning men, even when they deserved it, and even though her displays were masterful. I'd sensed a weakness in him, clenched my fist around it, and squeezed it like a ripe persimmon. However, Andre wasn't the one I needed to take down.

In class, I reflected on my life as Katarina. I enjoyed the wispy, baby-fine texture of my blond hair, but it fought the curling iron like Floyd Mayweather. Also, white hair smelled weird after two days, and washing could be a bit of a hassle. My ice-blue eyes were the best part. They were alien-beautiful. Almost impossible to think that a human could be blessed with the gift of the ocean in her eyeballs. If I had a glass eye, it would be blue. But as Toya, I had quarters and Mom and Dad and *Unsolved Mysteries*. And I had my brother.

By sixth period, the countdown to swim class was unbearable. I'd avoided Josh for days, but he was getting more difficult to dodge. The clock ticked faster than usual, and when the ocean waves started, my nerves kicked in. I toughened myself. If I could turn Andre to a six-foot pile of silent sludge, I could do anything.

I was the last one to get up from my desk, and when I walked toward the exit, Mr. Holder blocked the doorway with his arms folded.

"You've missed four rehearsals, missy." He made a show of tapping his powder-blue penny loafer.

"I'm sorry, I can't do show choir this year." I tried to get around him, but he propped his oversized hand on the door frame, effectively blocking my exit with his arm flab.

"You're my ingenue. My muse. My . . . my . . ." He tucked a stray hair behind my ear. "You're my Dolly."

"I'm just having some personal problems, Mr. Holder." I tried to get around him on the other side, and he threw his free arm against the opposite frame.

"I thought you might say something like that." He shook his head. "Teenagers, I tell y'all." He reached into the innermost pocket of his blazer and pulled out two discs. "Here."

I took the discs and flipped them over to see *DVD for My Dolly P.* written on one and *CD for My Dolly P.* written on the other.

"Parton?"

"The one and only."

I held them in the air. "Mr. Holder, I can't take these," I said, channeling my mother's resolve.

He placed his hands on my shoulders. "Listen here. I heard what they're saying about you. They're jealous bitches, the whole lot of them."

The curse word and the invasion of personal space caught me off guard.

"I want you, missy. Front and center." His eyes twinkled with desire.

"I know and I appreciate that. I just can't do it, not right now." I peeled his hands from my shoulders and placed the discs in his palm. "I can't be your Dolly. I'm sorry."

The ocean waves crashed again. I was late for swim.

The hall clock read 2:13, which meant everyone had already dressed out for the pool. To kill a little more time and collect my thoughts,

I stopped by the girls' room for a phantom pee. Once the latch met its mate, I realized I'd chosen the same bathroom stall that I'd eaten several lunches in as Toya. I knew because someone had written *#sluttybooboo* on the back of the door in red lipstick.

I'd asked God for so many unattainable things in that tiny space—friends, furniture, money, popularity, but mostly, I'd asked for Katarina. I looked down at my delicate fingers, still holding on to the clasp of the door. Those were the fingers I'd prayed for. I lifted them to my button nose and squeezed. That was the nose I'd prayed for. Anything but black, Lord, anything but black, never once considering what I was sacrificing in praying that prayer. Actually, I'm no fool, I knew exactly what I was sacrificing. I just didn't give a damn. Not about Dad's empty castle, or Mom's thrift stores.

Alex.

My knees gave out and I fell hard into a heap on the dirty stall floor. I began an unexpected *Braveheart*-worthy cry.

My built-in best friend. My knight in dingy T-shirts. My big brother was no longer mine. Now he was on his own, searching for quarters, eating whole McChickens, and chatting about life to himself.

The tears persisted. The hiccuppy, uncontrollable ones that babies do. I'd ignored all the disgusting pieces of myself for a while, and those were the tears that should've been cried on day one—when I was too busy picking out clothes and mixing with the worst sort of riffraff Edgewood High had to offer.

I pushed the stall door open with such force the uppermost hinge shattered, leaving it dangling and squeaking. I balled a tight fist, wheeled back, and punched the mirror, breaking Katarina's perfect reflection into tiny bloody shards.

FACING THE GIANTS

I slid my fingertips along the hallway walls, leaving tiny red specks on the smooth white drywall. Before entering swim, I peered through the cracked door to see the twins hugged up with Josh—Amera's hand hanging on his thigh and Amelia massaging his wet hair. His left eye was haloed by reddish-blue bruises and his bottom lip was double its size, but he still managed to smirk.

They're the worst. They'll break you if you let them. They'll draw you in, trip you up, and watch you fall flat on your face.

"Swim time," I said to myself.

I lifted my bloody hand to open the door, and my knuckles began throbbing. "No," someone's warm breath whispered over my right shoulder.

"I didn't call you," I told him. "This is a free-will situation. You can't stop me." I went to push the door again.

He placed his hand on top of my hand. "Just, no."

In a blink, we were in a 1990s-model Saab, merging onto the freeway. He smiled, shifting from fourth to fifth gear. The cassette player blasted the intro of Mariah Carey's "Always Be My Baby."

"Doo-doo-doop-dow," he sang off-key, and gave a quick glance in my direction. "Doo-doo-doop-doo-doop-doo-dow."

"Where the heck are we?" I said, shocked and a bit terrified.

"The freeway," he said, as if it were the most natural thing in the world to transport into a moving vehicle. "Buckle up."

I snapped my seat belt, taking it all in. The Saab smelled like old cracked leather and incense. Dirty coffee cups, Snickers wrappers, and miscellaneous trash littered the floorboards. The backseat was reserved for stacks of novels, including *The Catcher in the Rye*, *Slaughterhouse-Five*, and *Breaking Dawn*. Absolutely no sign of the Bible.

I reached for a book. "You read Twilight?" I asked, slightly amused.

He turned down Mariah. "Who hasn't?" He playfully snatched the book and tossed it over his shoulder. "Don't make fun, Toya. The Twilight Saga is outstanding."

I stared at him, speechless.

"Those books are popular for a reason," he said. "What?"

"It's just, I never imagined you having interests outside of, I don't know, saving people from sin and stuff. I mean, come on, Mariah Carey?" I asked, amazed. "Besides, Christians protested those books."

He grinned with a touch of contempt. "Christians are still human beings."

"I don't know. I guess I just imagined you reading . . ."

"The Bible?" he interjected.

"Yeah, that, and maybe C. S. Lewis or T. D. Jakes." I peered over my shoulder. "Certainly not *Slaughterhouse-Five*."

"I haven't read that one."

"What do you mean?" I asked. "It's right here in your backseat."

"Theoretically not my backseat."

"Wait just one doggone minute, now." I switched off Mariah Carey completely. "You stole a car?"

He involuntarily cut off the BMW in front of us. He rolled down the window, stuck out his head, and yelled, "I apologize!" He drew himself back into the car and grinned at me. "I really am getting better at driving."

"You're avoiding my question, Jesus."

"Yes, Latoya," he admitted. "I *borrowed* a car from someone who doesn't realize it's gone. But I will tell you with the utmost certainty that this person will not mind."

He looked at me, smiling, and the car drifted toward the shoulder.

"Curb alert!" I said—*boomph!*

"That curb came out of nowhere."

I laughed until my stomach hurt. "This is easily the most bizarre thing that's ever happened to me."

"Let's get off this freeway before it gets even more bizarre." He veered into the right lane, just missing a silver Honda, and exited into a gas station parking lot.

I placed my hands on the glove compartment, bracing for impact. "I hate to state the obvious, but you are a horrible driver."

"Ask yourself this, Latoya." He smiled. "Why on earth should I know how to drive?"

I nodded, because he was right and he knew it.

"Now." He pulled the brake and turned toward me. "What were you planning to say to Joshua and the twins?"

I really didn't have an answer for him. I pounded my head on the headrest. "I didn't have anything planned. I was just so . . . pissed. Sorry."

"Life is a difficulty." He flipped the visor and handed me a pair of Ray-Bans. "Bright eyes."

"Thanks for remembering," I replied. "Why does it have to be so hard?"

"The why lies in free will—the ability to choose which way to go and usually choosing . . ."

"Wrong?"

"No, Toya, never wrong. Very often the intention is spot-on. I've seen more commandments broken for the greater good than for frivolous reasons—murders to save loved ones, or theft to fill a child's hungry stomach. And in you, baby girl"—he tucked a stray strand of hair behind my ear—"more pain lives within you than in most."

I'd assumed everyone felt the way I felt. Hurt in the same ways that I'd hurt. I guess I'd assumed wrong.

"Your hurt pierces me." He pointed to his right side. "Here."

I slumped in my seat, dismayed. "But you've got, I don't know, billions of people to look after. People in real trouble. What makes me so special?"

He took a long, almost frustrated breath. "I never know how to explain such things. How about this: You're in a thrift store, searching for something special. You with me?"

"Uh, yeah," I said. "If there's one thing I know, it's thrift stores."

"Okay." He rubbed his hands together as if he was onto something. "You're in the mother of all thrift stores, larger than any you've ever seen before and filled to the brim with unique things. Then, out of nowhere, a spotlight shines in the back corner. You walk toward that spotlight because you have to. Your closest confidantes tell you to stay away, but you can't help it. You know that you're passing other great things, but in your heart, you feel something special is waiting there in the light."

"What's in the light?" I asked edgily.

"You."

"Me?"

"Self-deprecating, self-conscious, confused you. Staring up at me with those lovely brown eyes, asking for the power to change your perfect, beautiful self into something that you were never meant to be."

"Why'd you do it?"

"I've been asking myself that same question for many days now." He smiled.

"What do we do now, then?"

"Trust in me. Josh will be taken care of when the time is right." He glanced at the car's time display. "I have to get this car back to its rightful owner. And you"—he placed an index finger on my forehead—"back to the empty castle."

Hampton wagged his large tail and almost licked my face off. With one quick movement, I snatched a tick from his stomach. He let out a quick cry, and then began licking my palm to say thank you. That tick must've been bothering him for a while.

The empty castle felt emptier than usual. I trekked up the

stairs to my room and sat on the side of my twin bed. The brown spider that lived on my windowsill worked hard to create her evening masterpiece of a web. She was about a third of the way through, moving her eight legs with intentional chaos. I despised spiders with all my heart, and if she'd ever set foot inside my room, I wouldn't have hesitated to murder her, but behind the safety of the glass, I loved her. She was everything that I wanted to be: beautiful, independent, confident, strong, respected, intelligent, and fierce. Her body was the size of a quarter, not including the legs. All in all, for a spider, she was enormous.

"Jesus?" I turned around, but he wasn't there. "Jesus?" And nothing.

I woke to *Unsolved Mysteries* blaring downstairs. I skipped two steps at a time to join my family on the pillows. I stood on the fifth stair from the bottom, drinking in the view of my people. As usual, everyone got an oversized pillow to themselves. My designated pillow sat near the fireplace, awaiting my return. That episode of *Unsolved Mysteries* was the story about the ghost of Grace Brown. She was killed by Chester Gillette over a hundred years ago at the Covewood Lodge on Big Moose Lake, where she now haunted guests. One of my favorite episodes. When my weight shifted, the floor creaked beneath my feet. Alex's eyes never left the television. Mom and Dad, however, beamed at the sight of me.

"Toya!" said Mom.

"Hey, darling," said Dad, chewing on the wrong end of an ink pen.

I took a seat one and a half feet to the right of Alex, enough room to give him adequate space, but closer than we'd been in a while. Even before the fight, Alex and I respected each other's personal space. As a family, we had an unwritten knock-before-you-enter, lock-the-bathroom-door-behind-you, never-hug-too-long-or-sit-too-close policy.

The phone rang.

"I thought the phone was disconnected," said Alex. "Great job, Dad."

Dad beamed with pride.

"I'll get it." Mom popped up. "It's probably Evilyn. She hasn't been herself since some strange white girl took up for her in the park."

I sank deeper into my pillow.

"Hurry back." Dad waved the remote. "Grace Brown's ghost is about to take the lodge."

"I know," she replied. "Just a second."

They exchanged a weird look. Well, not a weird look for a regular married couple, but certainly for them. It was a tender look.

Alex didn't seem to notice.

"Toya!" Mom yelled from the kitchen. "Some boy is on the phone for you!"

Dad and Alex craned their necks in my direction. I slowly made my way to the kitchen. Mom held the phone out and whispered, "Someone named Dontay?"

"Oh!" I went to take the phone from her hand, and she lifted it out of my grasp.

"Who is Dontay?"

"Dee-on-tay, Mom," I pronounced, and then jumped for the phone.

"Well, excuuuuse me." She made her way back to the pillows.

"Hey," I said into the receiver.

"Hi," he replied. "I got your number from Ms. Wade. You still have a house phone?"

"Yeah." That was all I could say in response.

"Everything cool?"

"I never know what to say when people ask that. Is it a catchall, like how are you doing? Or should I really answer the question?" I knew I should've just said, *Yes, everything's cool.* But I had an irresistible longing to fill the dead space.

"Been a minute since I actually talked on the phone," he said. "I prefer text."

"I'm sure I would, too," I said, somewhat embarrassed. "I think we're the last family on the planet without access to a cell phone."

"It's cool, though. I like hearing your voice."

I'm certain my heart skipped a few beats on that one, but I couldn't think of anything to say in response. *I like hearing your voice, too? You're not as horrible as I thought you were? You're actually quite great? Your name made the back cover of my notebook?*

"Well, anyway," he said, finally. "Can I pick you up tomorrow morning at ten?"

"Sounds cool," I said, struggling to sound unaffected. "I'll be out front."

"See you then," he replied, also struggling to sound unaffected. "Bye."

"Okay, bye."

THE BAD SISTER

Mom and Dad turned the corner into the kitchen. They had been eavesdropping.

"What happens tomorrow?" asked Mom. "Your father and I have veto power."

"Is this supposed to be a date?" Dad inquired with wide-open eyes and blue ink on his lips.

"At ten in the morning? Surely not," I said, but they looked skeptical. "I mean, he didn't say it was or wasn't. I don't know. Should I call and ask him? How does it work?" I began pacing. "Oh God."

Dad grabbed me by the shoulders. "Look, doll. If a guy calls the night before to make sure you're showing up, it's definitely a date."

Mom did a double take. "Man! You been chewing on the front of an ink pen. Go wash up before you get lead poisoning."

"Ah, woman." Dad reluctantly stormed toward the downstairs bathroom.

Mom quietly watched him go. "Can we talk a minute?" Her voice softened.

I impulsively rolled my eyes. "Yes, Mom, can you make it—"

Before I finished my sentence, she was reaching for the car keys. "Come on before your dad sees."

Mom couldn't drive a stick shift, but she wasn't going to let that stop her. We jerked down Beckman Drive in horrified silence, while she concentrated on second and third gears versus neutral and fifth. When we reached the top of Colossus, she let out a sigh of relief and rode the brakes all the way down, eventually veering into Edgewood Park and shutting the engine off without shifting back into neutral. "I hate this car," I said.

"Me too, child," she said, and we laughed together for the first time in a while. "Nice evening."

The Alabama sky was streaked with a variation of ambers, darks blues, and purples. "Yeah, nice one."

Mom watched a woodpecker jabbing a telephone pole. "I wonder what he's looking for this time of night." We sat watching until he flew away.

"What's wrong, Mom?"

She still stared out her window, now watching a young white

couple teach their child to play tennis. She cleared her throat for a little longer than needed. "Well, I just wanted to take a minute to say something." She turned to me and reached her hand to my cheek. "You are so beautiful, baby girl."

"Mom, what's going on?" I asked, starting to feel panic.

She eased her hand away. "Your brother's going away for a little bit. He didn't want you to know, but I couldn't let him leave without you two figuring things out."

"What do you mean, going away for a little bit? When?"

"You know those letters?"

My heart did a little hop in my chest. "Yes, he's never told me what they are."

"They're recruiting him."

"Who?"

She turned back toward me. "Everyone, Toya. Harvard, MIT, Yale, Brown . . . all of them." She couldn't hold it in anymore. The tears began streaming down her face.

Really looking at her, I realized she'd been holding on by a thread for a while. Her soft hair flew from her head like flames, streaks of mascara lined her cheeks, and her hand was shaking a little. I don't know why I hadn't noticed before. My mother was on the verge of a nervous breakdown.

"How is that possible? He's absent just as much as I am. He must be failing, too."

"Your brother's not failing, Toya," she said deliberately. "He's actually doing well."

Come to think of it, I'd never asked him if he was failing. I'd assumed he was because I was. Even though he was absent as often as me, he'd chosen to push forward academically, quietly succeeding without making a fuss over himself. He could've bragged, but he didn't. He was dulling his own light so I wouldn't feel bad. He always protected me, even if he suffered for it.

"The letters aren't all he's been keeping from me," I said, mostly to myself.

"He started e-mailing the schools last year. He had an idea for something." She began shaking her head in confusion. "I don't understand it. It's way over my head." She slipped a letter from her purse. "You read it."

The paper was textured and off-white, with tiny speckles of gold hidden in the material, making it look more like fabric than paper. The burgundy emblem at the top left corner read *VE-RI-TAS* in three quadrants, with a white Harvard flag flying underneath the crest.

Dear Mr. Williams,

Thank you for sharing your comparison theory of social sensibility and terror management in

> impoverished communities. This illuminating
>
> model could shift the thinking of . . .

"Wait a minute," I said. "He applied to these schools without telling me?"

"No, baby." She placed her palm on my neck and began massaging slightly. "I think he was just sharing his thoughts with people who could understand them, and now they're recruiting him."

I skipped to the bottom.

> We would be exceedingly honored if you would
>
> tour the Department of Social Psychology within
>
> the College of Arts and Sciences, where we seek to
>
> understand human experiences and behaviors in
>
> social settings. We will gladly sponsor your trip . . .

I knew Alex was awesome, I just figured I was the only one who thought so. It had never crossed my mind that the rest of the world would ever recognize his awesomeness, too.

"When he was little, I had him tested, and he's a genius," Mom said slowly. "Toya, he's a genius. A real natural-born genius. He's in the high IQ club that President Obama and Sharon Stone are in. I can't think of the . . ."

"Mensa?"

"That's the one." She attempted to plug her flowing nostril with the knuckle of her index finger. "He never told us about the letters, because he knew we would encourage him to apply. He wanted to stay here, Toya." She looked over at me.

"Why?" I asked, though I already knew.

"He didn't want to leave you behind." She rummaged through the armrest for tissues and came up with a McDonald's napkin covered in special sauce. "But you've left him behind instead. I really can't believe it. I never would have believed it if I hadn't seen it for myself."

"I'm sorry."

"No, I understand why. It's my fault. Well, your father's, too, but mostly mine."

"What are you talking about, Mom?"

She looked at me like it should have been obvious. "I left you." She broke down into the most violent *Braveheart* cry I'd ever seen from her. "Really, I was leaving your father, but I left you guys, too. I shouldn't have done it, Toya. He's not even all that bad. He is pretty disgusting with the coffee, and I hate the junk cars, and that empty castle is a pitiful waste of money. But he loves you. He loves Alex. And—"

"He loves you, too, Mom. He told me as much."

"He did?"

"He did."

She pulled me into a forceful hug. The parking brake poked my ribs and she squeezed my neck so hard it hurt, but I stayed there. "I'm so sorry I left. You deserve a better mother than me, you both do, and I'm so sorry."

"It's okay, Mom." I just sat there and let her cry for what felt like a long time. I couldn't think of the words to comfort her. I figured she needed to confess and apologize. So I let her.

The semester my mom went to live with Aunt Evilyn, I'd gotten the worst progress report of my life, and I use the word *progress* lightly. I had earned seven straight Fs. I simply couldn't focus on algebra while Dad considered buying every crap car in the Gump. Or memorize state capitals while Mom refused to get out of bed at Aunt Evilyn's. I mean, who really cares about high school when your parents need wrangling? I worried about the stability of my household more than I'd ever concerned myself with school.

When Mom's waterworks finally calmed, I asked, "What school?"

She lifted her head from the wheel. "What?" she asked.

"What school is Alex going to?"

"That one." She pointed to the letter.

"Harvard?"

She nodded.

"How long will he be gone?"

"The whole summer, more if they love him, and of course they will." She drew a breath and blew her nose until the McDonald's napkin fell to pieces.

She opened the driver's-side door. "Let's go home."

"Wait, we're leaving the car here?"

"Not a chance in hell I'm getting this thing up that hill." She slammed the car door. "I'll send your daddy."

DEEP-DISH DIMPLE DEANTÉ

"Want your seats hot or cold?" asked Deanté as he opened the passenger-side door to his mother's Mercedes.

"It's eighty degrees today." I smiled. "Cold, obviously."

I ducked into the car and flipped the visor to check the mirror. When I saw my reflection in the lighted vanity mirror, the smile faded from my face. My cheeks and nose were splotched with pinpoint tiny red dots, and my eyes were puffy and dry from the awful night's sleep. When Deanté got in the driver's seat, I flicked the visor back up with more force than I'd intended.

Deanté turned in his seat. "Whoa. Did I do something already?"

"Can you just drive?" I asked, eager to escape Beckman Drive. As we drove I told Deanté about Alex's letters, Mensa, and my mom's breakdown in Edgewood Park. The truth poured from my lips, and Deanté stayed silent, listening intently and nodding where appropriate. It felt wonderful to speak without half-truths, or anxiety, just no-holds-barred truth telling for the first time in weeks. I spoke so fast that I couldn't keep up with myself. After unloading my family problems, I exhaled loudly and slouched in my seat.

"I'm sorry," I said. "This is a horrible way to start our date."

"Wait," he said, beaming. "Is this a date?"

"Deanté!" I shouted. "From everything I just said, is that all you heard?"

"Nah, I was listening to you. I just don't really know what to say. You know what I mean? I can't say I'm surprised that Alex is legit Mensa-level smart. Everybody knows he's got a little something extra going on."

I could tell he was cautiously forming his words so as not to offend, so I decided to let him off the hook. "Well," I said. "Thanks for listening anyway. It helps to talk about it out loud."

"Anytime," he replied. "Oh, and we're here." We were underneath the arched entryway of the campus of Alabama State University. "You ever been here?"

"I live in Montgomery, Deanté. Of course I've been to ASU," I said, feeling uneasy. Alabama State was an HBCU—a historically black college/university—and when I say I'd been to ASU, I actually meant I'd ridden past it on the way to Edgewood. I'd never actually left the car and entered any of the buildings.

"My bad, dang. I asked because a lot of Edgewood folks don't leave the neighborhood. Some of my old homies have never seen the inside of an ASU building." Deanté was positively sunny as we rode past the stadium. "Welcome to Hornet Nation, Toya." He smiled over at me.

"Thanks," I said. "But why exactly are we here?"

He made a parking space in front of a fire hydrant. "I thought about our conversation after Josh . . . you know," he said.

"Yes, I know. Go on."

"You asked me why I acted so black, remember?" He paused. "I couldn't think of an answer. All that mess about choosing hard-core black instead of being an Oreo, that was bullshit. It bothered me that I couldn't explain, so after I dropped you off, I came here."

"I'm not sure I understand, Deanté."

"Just . . . no one's ever had the balls to ask me that question, not even my boys—and they're supposed to be hard." He shook his head. "I've been trying to explain it to myself, more than anything, why I treated your brother like that. And you . . ." He shifted in his seat, obviously uncomfortable. "I made you . . . hell . . . I still don't know why I did that sick shit with the Jordans."

"It's okay."

"It's really not," he said, not allowing me to let him off the hook this time. "Just so you know, I've always appreciated your style. You and Alex. Y'all don't fall in line like the rest of us. You do your own damn thing and I respect that. I just never had the guts to admit it." He pulled from the parking space. "I want to show you something."

Rolling through campus, I realized it'd never crossed my mind to visit ASU. "When I came here the night of the party, this is what I saw." He pointed to a brown-skinned girl sitting alone on the grassy quad. She wore plaid parachute pants, a bright orange head scarf, and a T-shirt that read *Screw Normal* in multicolored letters. He placed his palm on my knee. "It's you." He smiled.

"And Alex," I replied.

"Yeah. Him too."

Students crisscrossed the sidewalks and streets, blocking the car from progressing too far past the stadium. Most of the students wore black-and-gold T-shirts reading something like *Hornet Nation* or *When We Teach Class, the World Takes Note*. I noticed all shades of black people from nearly passable light-skinned to deep dark mahogany. They were all headed in the same direction.

"Where are they all going on a Saturday?"

"That's the surprise," he replied. "What time is it?"

I looked down at my watch. "Almost eleven."

"Dang, I'll just park here," said Deanté, as he spun the wheel, parking half on and half off the sidewalk.

"I told you that I don't really like surprises. What's going on?"

Deanté put the car into park and shifted toward me. "Okay, I have to be quick because it's about to start. Do you know my sister, Andrea?"

"I know of her. She was a senior when I was a freshman," I said, more confused than before.

"She goes here, and her probate show is today." He grinned ear to ear.

After a pause, I said, "I give up. What's a probate show?"

Deanté squeezed his cell phone. "Shoot! We're about to miss it. Let's go."

Everyone was headed to Lockhart Gym to see this probate show. The closer we got to the building, the more I noticed the pink balloons tied to cars, and poles, and benches, and anything else that would stand still. When we reached the building, we were greeted by an enormous banner reading GAMMA PI INTRODUCING: THE FAIR FORTY.

"Forty what?" I whispered into Deanté's ear.

"There are forty Neos on the line. My sister is the Tail-Dog," he said, still grinning.

"What's a Neo?" I asked.

"Toya, honestly, have you ever been on this campus before?"

I shook my head.

"I suspected as much," he replied, pointing toward two of the last empty seats. When he grabbed my hand, I nearly leaped from my skin. I looked around to make sure there would be no Gus Von March–type encounter, but to my surprise, no one paid us any mind. Everyone was talking, laughing, and minding their own business. When I calmed down and looked at our fingers tangled together, butterflies flipped my diaphragm. When we reached the seats, he didn't let go of my hand.

"Okay, I'll give you a brief rundown of what's happening here. Gamma Pi is a member of the National Black Council for black Greek organizations. There are nine total, but only four are all-female. Follow me?" When I nodded, he kept going. "Andrea's always wanted to be GP because my mom pledged back in the eighties. When they accepted her back in January, she called me screaming, so excited."

"Wait. If she got accepted back in January, why does the sign say they're being introduced today?" I asked.

"Great question," he said, then looked around to make sure no one was listening. "That's how long it takes to pledge GP. There's a process. Andrea told me a little about it, but most of it is secret stuff that no one outside of the sorority knows."

"Wow," I said, just noticing the blocked-off section taking up the first three rows of the auditorium. I nudged Deanté. "Is that them?"

"No, they're Prophytes, or big sisters. They always wear white on probate day. Cool, huh?" he asked, still squeezing my hand.

Sitting on his left side, I saw his dimple peeking through. "Yes, Deanté. Very cool."

Out of the blue, the audience began to stir, and an earsplitting screech pierced the chatter of the crowd. After a moment, I realized that sound was coming from the ladies in white. I plugged my ears. "What are they doing?"

Deanté drew my hands from my ears. "That's their call. Every sorority and fraternity has one."

"Oh," I said, feeling stupid.

He squeezed my hand again. "You had no way of knowing," he said, flashing that dimple. "Look!"

He pointed to the stage, where two of the ladies in white walked toward the standing microphone. They were both average build with pixie haircuts, but one towered over the other.

"Welcome all to the coming-out ceremony of the finest line you've ever seen in your life!" All Prophytes rose to their feet and hollered at the two girls, encouraging them. "I'm Laquita, the DP of the Forty," said the tall girl.

"And I'm Jamitria, the ADP," said the shorter of the two.

Without my having to ask, Deanté whispered in my ear. "DP stands for dean of pledges. She's in charge of them while they're on line. ADP is assistant dean of pledges, and she stands in when the DP can't make it."

I smiled. "Thank you."

"Quita? You think they're ready to meet our girls?" asked Jamitria.

"Nah, Jam. They couldn't be ready," replied Laquita.

As if on cue, everyone in the audience stood to their feet, including myself and Deanté. "Are y'all ready for our girls?" Laquita asked the spectators. In response, the auditorium roared and yelled with excitement.

"If you're ready, make some noise!" said Jamitria.

Jamitria and Laquita stepped off the stage and the Prophytes began to chant.

You're my,

Gamma Pi,

I'm yours,

Gamma Pi.

As long as I live,

My heart I will give,

You know why,

My Gamma Pi.

You know why,

My Gamma Pi.

They repeated the mantra five times and let out a collective call. Then forty masked girls, ordered by height, marched onto the stage. They were dressed identically in pink cocktail dresses.

"Pink is their trademark," whispered Deanté. "You see the tail-dog?"

"Is that like their mascot?"

Deanté chuckled. "No, tail-dog means the tallest one on the line. The one in the back, Andrea."

"Oh, sorry," I said.

Andrea marched with so much control that she stood out from the rest. "She's amazing."

"Yeah, I know." Deanté looked proudly at his big sister, and I thought about Alex. He hadn't told me about the letters because I didn't deserve to know. I didn't support him like Deanté supported Andrea. I relied on him to protect me and be my best friend when no one else would, but I didn't support him like that. The thought of my brother leaving me hurt—bad. I knew that I had absolutely no right to feel that way, but I couldn't help it. He was like the strawberry jelly on my sausage biscuit; it would just be wrong without him, speaking terms or otherwise.

"Hey." Deanté shook at my arm. "You okay?"

I forced a smile. I didn't want to ruin this for him. "Yeah. Your sister is the best one up there!"

"Shhh, keep your voice down." He grinned. "We're not supposed to know who she is until she takes the mask off."

The show began with the reciting of the Greek alphabet. All forty Neos said the words so quickly that all I could make out was alpha at the beginning and omega at the end. Afterward they greeted the fraternities with skits and songs, saving the longest greeting for their brother fraternity, Gamma Phi.

"A lot of Gamma Pi girls date Gamma Phi boys," Deanté said, staring at the section of guys wearing white-and-gold suits, vests, and bow ties. "That's what I'm going to be one day."

In response to their extended greeting, Gamma Phi held two fingers in the air and recited a chant of their own, right from the audience.

We love our,

Our Gamma Pi,

We wife our,

Our Gamma Pi.

What is Gamma Phi,

Without Gamma Pi?

We love our lovely Gamma Pi.

Their deep voices in contrast to Gamma Pi's high-pitched song gave me chills.

"Look at that, Toya." Deanté smiled. "Nobody's telling them how to act or who to be. But still they choose bow ties and suits. One day, Toya, one day." His eyes were fixed on Gamma Phi.

"I can see why you'd want to be one of them," I said to Deanté.

Afterward one girl broke from the other forty—Deanté's sister. She began stomping and stepping in the center of the stage while the other thirty-nine girls formed a giant G behind her. Their synchronized hand and foot movements were impressive, but everyone's eyes fell on Andrea. She was magnetic. When they completed the formation, all forty girls lined up, again by height.

"We are the fantastic Forty, the phenomenal Forty, the soul-stepping Forty of Gamma Pi," they said as one. "Now it's time to reveal ourselves."

"They're about to take off the masks," said Deanté, barely containing his excitement. "They'll start with the shortest in line, or the Ace."

As if on cue, the shortest girl stepped forward from the line and ripped her mask off. The exhilarated crowd roared so loudly that I had to strain to hear her introduction. "My name is Carmen Riley from Tuscaloosa, Alabama, and I am the Ace of this line!" She stepped back and the second girl marched forward.

"My name is Jasmine Sanders from Atlanta, Georgia!" She flipped her hair and stepped back as well.

The introductions went rather quickly. The variation of black women on that stage was striking. Some light-skinned with long curly hair, some as dark as ebony with stylized buzz cuts, others with micro-braids, even a few were my original color—the color of coffee with a single hit of cream. The girls on that stage were so different from the girls at Edgewood High School. Not just because they were black, but because they were free to express their individuality to the world without fear of judgment. Really, it was more than that: The crowd applauded their uniqueness. No one sniggered at the ones with ethnic names, or unstraightened hair, or thicker bodies. Just then, I understood why fate led Deanté to ASU the night of the party, and in turn, why he'd led me.

Deanté elbowed me. "Andrea's next."

When Andrea yanked off her mask, the audience went wild. I could tell she was well-known, and well-liked, from the tremendously positive response. A girl standing behind us said, "She's in my biology lab. I love her!"

Deanté turned around and bragged, "She's my sister."

"My name is Andrea Evans from Montgomery, Alabama, and I am the Tail-Dog of this line!"

When all masks were off, the crowd roared and the Prophytes screeched their last call.

The crowd began to disperse. "You ready?" asked Deanté.

I nodded, but I was not.

On the way to my house, Deanté drove with his left hand and held my hand with his right. I kept playing the probate over and over in my mind. The unity in the auditorium. The beautiful variation of the ladies on the stage. Deanté's undeniable pride for his sister. I needed to tell Alex about it.

When I got home, I shot upstairs to Alex's room and knocked on his door. "Alex!" I shouted. "Can we pause our . . . our fight for a bit? I have something to tell you."

The door cracked. He peeked through the opening; his face was creased from sleeping on his side. "What is it?"

"I went to Alabama State today. I actually got out of the car and went into a building. And you won't believe—"

"Not interested." He eased the door shut. "I'm going back to sleep."

CHURCH ON THE MOUNTAIN

I thought I was dreaming. Then Mom's yelling became more pronounced and I knew that I certainly was not. "Everybody! Get up!"

There was a ferocious pounding on my bedroom door, followed by a knock on Alex's. "Nobody's missing church this morning."

When I glanced at the clock, it read 6:47. What she actually meant was nobody's missing morning prayer, Sunday school, or church service.

"Jesus, help," I said to the ceiling.

"With?" He passed my sunglasses.

"How am I supposed to go to church with them?" I inquired, shocked that he even had to ask. "This is Mount Mariah Baptist

we're talking about. Everyone knows us, and they'll definitely notice that I don't belong."

He held his magic index finger in the air. "Wait for it. . . ."

Another bang on my door. "We're going to that new church
everyone's talking about. That big one off the freeway called Church
on the Mountain."

He smiled.

And so did I.

The church was an hour away, and quite literally on the top of a
mountain. It was the first megachurch I'd seen in real life. The
line of cars exiting the freeway held up the right lane for nearly a
mile and a half. As we sat there waiting, Mom and Dad kept looking at each other.

"Your shirt isn't too wrinkled," Mom said softly.

Dad cheesed in response. "I ironed it."

"You did an okay job, too." She reached for the back of his
collar and gave it a tug. "There."

Dad looked away. "I like your crown," he said into the steering wheel.

Mom flipped down her visor. "It turned out good, didn't it? I
tried an under-braid this time. I like it better than over-braid."

It really did look beautiful. She'd braided her fluffy hair into
an uninterrupted hair-crown, leaving two strategically separated

tendrils cascading down the back of her neck. If there was a black woman in Greek mythology, my mother would be the physical manifestation.

I leaned into Alex. "Mom told me about Harvard."

Mom and Dad turned to glare at me, while Alex glowered at Mom. "I told you not to tell her!"

"I couldn't help myself," Mom said. "She can't just not know that her brother is leaving the state. That's cruel."

"She's cruel!" he screamed.

"Don't say that, Alex," Mom and Dad said in unison.

"He's right" was all I could think to say. "He's right."

The Fiat stalled as the church line began moving, and everyone's attention diverted to the engine. Together, we encouraged it to come alive. It wouldn't, and the horns started blaring. Mom leaped from the car in her flowered tea-length chiffon dress and placed her hands on the trunk, ready to push. I let up the seat and took my place at her flank.

"Sorry for tattling on you," I said.

She caressed my head and smiled. "I knew you would."

Then Alex slipped out and scooched between us. It was the first time he'd made contact with me since our fight.

"All right, Dad," he ordered. "Steer!"

Dad piloted us onto a grassy knoll on the side of the highway. The Christians rolled past us; one pickup truck driver gave us the finger on his way to church. We squished back into the Fiat and Dad tried and tried to turn the engine over. But the car showed no sign of life.

"We should pray," Mom said. "All heads bowed, eyes closed."

Alex looked at her, half smiling, before squeezing his eyes shut.

"Oh, Dear Heavenly Father, touch this Fiat with your loving hands, God. Give it life in the name of Jesus. Bring this car back to life in the mighty name of Jesus."

Peeking, I saw Alex's shoulders bouncing from silent laughter, Dad embracing the steering wheel like a mother would hug a small child, and Mom asking God to save the car's life. I burst out laughing. I couldn't help it.

"This is serious, child," Mom said, which only made Alex and me laugh more fiercely. Then she joined in.

Dad was the last to join, and when he did, the tiny car rocked from the force of our united laughter. I can imagine how insane we looked in the broken-down convertible on the side of the street. To the onlookers I didn't belong, but inside the confines of the Fiat, I was an essential piece. We were family, and in that rare moment, none of us cared what anyone outside that car thought. Everything that could go wrong was going wrong, and what else was there to do but laugh?

When we all settled down, Dad clapped his hands and said, "Looks like we're walking."

"Wait, Dad." I smiled. "Give it one more try."

Dad paused for a moment, closed his eyes, and then turned the key.

The Fiat came alive.

"How did you know?" Dad asked.

I shrugged as if I didn't know, but really, Jesus had just removed his hand from the hood of the car.

Walking from the car to the church felt like walking into the mouth of a living organism. Golf carts snaked the parking lot, offering rides from parking spaces to the front door. Greeters waited at every entrance, shaking hands and high-fiving patrons. There were even baristas standing near the coffee stations, offering attendees a cup on the house. Even though everyone was kind and welcoming, the church felt very . . . mega.

"I don't know, Dad," whispered Alex.

Dad was pouring himself a cup of free church coffee. "Yeah, I don't know, either, son."

Mom cupped her hand around Dad's waist. "Golden Corral instead?"

"You read my mind," Dad replied. "GC it is." He pointed to the exit.

We loaded back into the Fiat as the worship team began belting "The Great I Am." The harmony was beautiful, magical even, but we instantly knew the Church on the Mountain wasn't for us. Mount Mariah Baptist certainly had its flaws—an aged preacher, judgmental church mothers, off-key hymns led by the same bogarting showboat soprano who just happened to be the head deacon's granddaughter. But Alex and I were both christened in that tiny church. I'd spilled my first Communion on the crimson carpet—if you squint hard enough, you can still make out the stain. Most important, Mom and Dad were married at the base of the pulpit. There would be no replacing Mount Mariah.

On the way to GC, Mom touched Dad's leg six and a half times—the final time she'd caught me watching and pulled back with a wink. When we arrived, GC was still serving breakfast, which is a few dollars cheaper than lunch and way more delicious. I caught sight of the waitress from our last GC outing. She was a squirrelly woman with stringy, bleached hair and cigarette fingers. She saw my family and then she scrambled to the waitress-keep, I assumed to tell her friends to steer clear of the gratuity-dodging black family that just walked through the door.

I hung back so as not to draw attention from the cashier, but when Dad announced, "Four buffets, please," the cashier replied with "Three buffets?" And then Dad said, "Four, please." And again the cashier said, "You mean three." And Mom interrupted with "The man said four buffets, are you deaf?"

"Mom, will you come with me to the bathroom?" I whispered to her.

The crowd was thick on the way to the ladies' room. When we finally made it, the line twisted out the door.

"Can you hold it?" she asked. "I'm ready to eat."

"No, Mom," I replied, glad the line was long. I needed to talk to her. "What's going on with you and Dad?"

"Oh, Lord have mercy, gal." She flailed her arms around uneasily. "You need to stay out of grown folks' business."

"I think it's sweet."

She looked straight into my eyes. "You do?"

"I do."

"He ironed his shirt," she said, fiddling with her chiffon dress.

"And he's been better with the coffee."

"I know!" She jumped and nearly tipped me over.

"He's trying so hard," I added. "I'm glad you see it."

"Are you in line?" a woman interrupted. A gap had formed in front of us while we were talking.

"Oh, yeah." Mom hurried to fill the break in the line. She skipped forward, her feet catching air on every step. My mother reminded me of so many girls in my classes—positively giddy over a boy.

And I thought of Deanté.

❖ ❖ ❖

Dad and Alex had chosen a booth in the back corner. They'd already fixed their plates, but they hadn't started eating yet.

"Just look at them," Mom said with pride. "Waiting patiently to pray with us before they take a bite."

Alex motioned us to come to the table, in the process nearly knocking over his ice water. "Doesn't look too terribly patient to me, Mom."

We sat down across from them. "Who's praying?" Dad asked.

"Alex," Mom simply replied.

Alex's face went from hungry impatience to total shock.

Dad placed his hand firmly on Alex's shoulder. "You can do it, kiddo."

It seemed like a small thing, but in our house, it was not. Prayer around a table of food in the Williams household was done by the adults. For Alex to be asked meant respect.

We held hands over the table and closed our eyes, preparing for Alex's first family prayer. It felt like a monumental moment. Like, after Alex began speaking, he would cross some invisible line into adulthood.

"Dear heavenly—" he started.

"Can I get y'all something else other than water?" asked cigarette hands. "We got orange juice, lemonade, sweet tea, caw-fee . . ."

230

I could feel the heat rising from Mom's skin. I sensed a scene. I could tell that Alex sensed it, too.

"No, thank you," Alex said sweetly. "We're just about to—"

"Well, I'm fixin' to go on break," she interrupted.

Mom's nostrils flared like an uncontrolled bull.

"If you know what's good for you," Dad told the waitress, "you'll stop interrupting my son's prayer and leave this family be."

The waitress locked eyes with me like our mutual blondness made us allies against them. When she didn't find what she was looking for in my eyes, she flipped her stringy hair and stormed off.

Mom's nostrils relaxed and her heat began to cool. "All right, Alex."

It was the perfect prayer, like Alex had been practicing for years to get it just right. He covered us all—Mom, Dad, Hampton, Aunt Evilyn, and me. Mostly me. The four of us shed many tears together in that GC booth.

The ride home was mostly quiet. Smiling, chuckling, praying Alex had disappeared and melancholy Alex had returned, but at least I knew he was still in there.

Alex needed me. Mom needed me. Dad needed me. Deanté

wanted me. Or at least it seemed so. It was time to do something for them. It was time to be there for the most important people in my life. It was time to do the right thing for the first time in a while.

I needed to ask God for one last thing.

LOOSE ENDS?

On Monday morning, the unfortunate world of Edgewood High seeped back into my consciousness. It was getting harder to ignore the whispers and STD jokes. I wanted to leave. I wanted to disappear into the bathroom stall at lunchtime, but I needed to face the twins as Katarina. More important, I had to confront Josh through the same blue eyes he'd tried to violate. I couldn't take the coward's way out and run like I usually did.

"Alex hates you, you know that, right?" I asked Deanté as he leaned against his locker, one ankle crossed over the other. He was wearing the Jordans.

"I don't know what to do about that."

"You don't know what to do about that, or you don't care enough to try?"

He reached for my arm and I snatched it away.

"Everything okay?" asked a male teacher walking by.

I turned my back to the teacher before rolling my eyes. "Of course everything's fine."

He walked away, looking skeptical. "Toya," Deanté whispered. "You can't do stuff like that. Not when you're still . . . you know. I could get in real trouble in this town. Damn."

"I know." I turned to him. "I shouldn't've."

"What's wrong with you anyway? You're acting, I don't know, different."

I looked down at his shoes.

"Oh," he said, before kicking them off.

"What are you doing? You can't walk around school barefoot. Put them back on."

He ignored my request, walked to the trash can, and threw them in. When he realized everyone had stopped to watch, he marched toward a tiny, terrified freshman boy holding a McDonald's coffee cup. "Hey, kid, can I have the rest of that coffee?"

"Hot chocolate," the boy said, nervously handing it over.

Deanté mussed his hair. "Thanks," he said before lifting the lid from the trash can and pouring the hot drink all over his Jordans. "I'd rather be barefoot than hurt you again."

I felt the heat rising in my face. "I appreciate that more than you'll ever know."

Deanté looked ashamed and proud at the same time. "I have to run to the pool. I think Miss Baker has those plastic shower shoes. See you later?"

I nodded. "Definitely." I saddled my backpack and went to Mrs. Roseland's history fifteen minutes early.

I heard Alex's distinct cry as I approached Mrs. Roseland's cracked classroom door. His cries sounded like computer glitches— every word separated by a labored gulp of air. I grabbed my chest and eased toward the opening to listen.

"I'm . . . just . . . not . . . sure . . . Mrs. . . . . Rose . . . land."

"There, there, there, Alexander." Mrs. Roseland's deep Southern drawl was famous for calming kids. "I know you're scared, but you'll look back over this decision and thank your lucky stars you chose to leave. This isn't the place for you. And all the work you've done. I knew that reaching out to Harvard would pay off. I promise, up there you won't have to pretend to fit in, you just will. Imagine a world where everybody's as brilliant as you are. Where you don't have to explain things to people. You'll love it, love it, love it."

"I . . . know . . . but . . . what . . . about . . . Toya?"

"Toya's off on her own adventure." I could hear Mrs. Roseland's smile. "It's your turn."

"I know you're right." Alex blew his nose.

"Have I ever told you about my summer in New Orleans?" she

shouted over his honking nose. "Well, I realize this might be hard to believe, but Alabama history is not my passion." She paused for a reaction, but Alex stayed quiet. "Anyway, high school was a challenge for me. I was different, too. Not book bright, like you, but creative."

"What kind of creative?"

"I'm a painter," she said with sadness in her voice. "Never sold anything. Not for money anyway. Once I traded a life-size portrait for a discount on my summer air-conditioning. I doubt that counts for selling."

I wanted Alex to ask what she'd done in New Orleans.

"What did you do during your summer in New Orleans?" he asked as I finished my thought, and my chin began to vibrate. We were so much alike.

"I painted, my boy." Mrs. Roseland sighed. "My mother's mother lived right there on the bayou, her deck overlooking the tail of Lake Pontchartrain. She set up an easel and let me alone all summer. Just me, the canvas, and the water. Best summer of my life so far."

"So why aren't you a painter, then?"

"Well, well, well," she said. "That's the summer I had my little girl."

"Oh, I'm sorry, Mrs. Roseland," he sputtered. "I shouldn't pry. . . ."

"Don't you be sorry," she said sweetly. "I'm not. I gave up my dreams for the sake of my daughter, and I'd do it again. You, Alexander Williams, are a shining star like none I've ever seen. But the door won't stay open too much longer, not even for you. Walk through it, you hear me?"

"Yes, ma'am," he said, accepting her charge.

That's when I realized that Alex had his own guide. Not Jesus, but the next best thing. Sweet, quirky Mrs. Roseland.

"Now get to ISS before that stupid ocean catches you," she teased.

I heard his footsteps nearing the door, and I hid behind an open locker. I wanted to call after him, but by the time I'd gathered enough courage, the moment had passed.

Miss Baker had the flu, so swim class relocated to the practice field bleachers. I snuck in and sat behind the twins so they couldn't see me arrive. I wanted to be brave but I wasn't dumb enough to put myself on exhibit. When I was within earshot, I realized they were talking about Josh and his ex-girlfriend, Ashley Hemphill.

"OMG, did you hear?"

"What?"

"OMG!"

"What?"

"So, okay . . . OMG!"

"OMG! *What?*"

"I heard Ashley had a baby last year——"

"OMG!"

"*Yeah!* That's why she didn't start school until after Christmas break, because she had Josh's baby, and his dad made her give it up for adoption. That's why they gave her the Prius. To shut her up about the baby." My composition notebook slipped from my hands, skipped two sets of bleachers, and fell on one of their heads.

"Ouch!" Amera said.

"I hope there's no sexually transmitted stuff on the notebook," said Amelia before kicking it away.

"I know, right?"

"Even if there were, it would be *sexually* transmitted," I said under my breath.

They turned away, eager to carry on their juicy gossip. "So, how did you find out?" asked Amera, focusing Amelia's attention back to her.

"Turns out that Ashley wanted to keep the baby so badly she went back to the adoptive parents' house and demanded that they let her see it. . . ."

"OMG!"

"They live on Rainbow, a few streets over from her!"

"OMG!"

"She banged on the door screaming, and when they called the police, Stephen's dad was the cop on duty. How lucky is that? Stephen texted me last period to tell me. . . ."

"You should let him see both boobs for that spicy news!" They laughed.

But I couldn't hold it any longer.

"I don't see anything funny," I interjected.

They slowly turned to face me. "What did you just say to us?"

"I said . . ." I stood over them. "I don't think it's funny to run your big mouths about people who are in real trouble."

"How dare . . ." Amera tried to stand, but I pressed her shoulders until she was seated again. "Hey. That hurts."

"That's the point," I said, millimeters from her nose.

Amelia sat silently with terror in her eyes.

"You know what else isn't funny?" I screeched, making sure everyone in the bleachers could hear me. "Calling Jim the *R* word, and spreading disgusting rumors, and using racial slurs! You should both be ashamed of yourselves. You vapid, pathetic, sad excuses for human beings."

Walking Edgewood High School's hallways that afternoon was the hardest thing I'd done in a while. Everyone watched with fear and adoration, as if I'd brought down the undefeatable two-headed beast. But really, they were tiny and sad. I'd expected a fight from them. I was, after all, outnumbered; but they just sat there and listened to my lecture like two toddlers in time-out. It was like they were waiting for someone to put them in their place.

"I'm proud of you." It was Deanté.

"Is it all around school?" I asked, knowing full well the answer was yes.

"You mean Ashley's pregnancy or your badassness?" he asked.

"Both?"

"Both." He slipped his arm around my waist. "That's sad what happened to Ashley, though. Real talk."

"He'll probably get away with it, too," I said, feeling sick to my stomach.

"Not if I have anything to do with it." I nearly leaped from my skin at the sound of my brother's voice. His face was beet-red and fuming.

"Listen, dude," Deanté said before removing his hand from my waist and taking a small step back. "Josh ain't worth getting expelled over. You already kicked his ass raw."

I couldn't speak. It was as if an alien had landed in the semicircle between Deanté and myself. My big brother had spoken to me. Spoken to *Deanté*!

"We have to get him," Alex said through his teeth.

"We?" I whispered.

"First, I have to ask," he said to a visibly shaken Deanté. "What are your intentions with my little sister?"

Deanté fell into an indecipherable sputter. There were positively no salvageable words.

"I've been watching you." Alex held his hand out to shake, and Deanté took it. "Nice move with the Jordans."

"How did you . . . ?" I started.

"ISS is a hack," he said openly. "The teacher changes every day. One day they let the narcoleptic media center lady watch us. Mostly I've walked the halls. It's basically the Monday through Friday version of *The Breakfast Club.*"

"You don't hate me, then?"

"I could never hate you, Toya." He swiped a tear from my cheek. "I forgave you at GC."

I clinched him into the biggest, longest bear hug. I didn't care who saw. My brother was mine again. He wore an off-white T-shirt that used to be white, and too-big beige corduroys in the heat of late spring. He smelled like a three-way tie between McDonald's, Hampton, and woodsy outside.

"All right, stop this," he said, gently pulling away from the hug. "We have more pressing matters to tend to."

"Josh?" Deanté asked.

"Josh," Alex answered, more self-assuredly than I'd ever heard him. "And I know just what to do."

He flashed a double-big bottle of MiraLAX in his book bag.

"I've been saving my quarters."

I snatched it from his hands. "This is the biggest bottle of laxative I've ever seen in my life." I shook it. "What are you—?"

"Slip it in his protein shake," he said matter-of-factly. "He drinks one every morning."

"Am I missing something?" inquired Deanté. "How are we supposed to get it into his drink without him noticing?"

"That's the brilliant part." Alex shook the bottle. "It's powder." He ogled us as if expecting excitement. He got confusion instead.

"I don't get it," I said, completely oblivious.

"The protein mix is powder, too," he added. "We dump half and replace it. He won't know what hit him. I mean, he will but it will be too late."

Deanté and I smirked at each other, just beginning to understand.

"But wait." I realized there was a giant hole in his plan. "How do we get access to the protein mix?"

Alex tucked the bottle back into his bag. "Josh left his locker combination sticker on the back of his lock."

"So damn dumb." Deanté shook his head.

"Beyond dumb," Alex agreed.

I chimed in. "He deserves to crap his pants just for being that dumb."

The three of us laughed together for the first time ever. Hopefully not the last.

The stage was set for the most epic takedown anyone had ever seen at Edgewood High School. Most Edgewood kids drove their own cars, and others waited in the drop-off for their parents to pick them up, so the lower floors were quiet. We hid near the locker rooms as the school emptied out. Deanté kept watch near the stairwell, and Alex and I waited by the doors for his all clear.

"Thanks for forgiving me, Alex."

"Will you stop saying that?" He was getting annoyed with me. "And keep your voice down."

"I really am sorry for everything, though."

"Latoya Williams," he started. "Wait, I think that's the all-clear signal."

"No, I think he was legitimately scratching his head."

"The signal was a pat, not a scratch," Alex countered. "He patted."

"No, Alex. Look."

Deanté thrashed his arms around at us, exasperated that we hadn't read his signal.

"Told you it was a pat." Alex gently pressed the boys' locker room door. "Let's do this."

The boys' locker room was the mirror image of the girls'. The only major difference was it smelled like sweaty crotch that hadn't been washed in weeks.

I shielded my face with my arm. "What *is* that?"

"Jockstrap." Deanté crept behind us.

"You're supposed to be watching the stairs," Alex snapped.

"I wasn't about to miss this masterpiece," Deanté answered. "Nobody's up there."

We followed Alex to the back corner of the locker room.

Alex stopped in front of number 262, a floor-length gray locker covered in dents and dings. Alex pulled the MiraLAX from his bag and began opening the bottle with his teeth. "One of you, open the lock."

"I'll do it." I flipped the lock and there it was, faded but readable. "Remember this, Deanté. Twelve, seventeen, thirty-three."

"Twelve, seventeen, thirty-three, got it."

I took a breath before twisting the lock three times to the twelve. Then I spun twice to seventeen and finally thirty-three. *Click.*

"All right." Alex lifted the bright red, basketball-sized jug of protein powder from the floor of Josh's locker. He twisted the shiny silver lid. "Hold this." He handed me the laxative, pried the lid from the steel trash can, and dumped the majority of the protein powder from the container.

"Now." He looked from me to Deanté and back to me. "Pour."

And so I did.

SIMPLY DEANTÉ

The next morning, Alex could hardly sit still in the backseat from anticipation of things to come. I was nervous, though. I thought of Josh's retribution when all I'd done was tell the twins about his swim snot. I could only imagine what he'd do with MiraLAX-level embarrassment.

"Bye, Mom. Bye, Dad." Alex bounded from the Fiat and headed to the ISS wing. "Bye, Toya." He gave me a quick side-hug.

Mom and Dad beamed at us before sputtering away.

"Today's going to be big." Deanté stood in the school breezeway. "You must be scared as hell."

I smiled. "It's not even first period yet. How is it that you already know everything about me?"

"How many times do I have to tell you? Nothing happens at this school without me knowing about it." He winked.

"Who do you have first period?" I asked.

"Howard," he replied. "Why?"

"I've got Roseland. You don't think they would notice if we skip out, do you?" Roseland might not, but Mrs. Howard certainly would.

His eyes widened. "Oh, they won't notice." Liar. I was testing him to see if he wanted alone time as badly as I did, and there it was.

I'd never imagined myself walking to the practice fields alone with Deanté. The practice fields had a bit of a reputation—it was *the* place to make out. As we walked, he kicked at the dirt and held his hands in his pockets.

"When are you planning on changing back anyway?" he asked a bit too eagerly.

"Tomorrow, I think," I said, wondering if it would be that easy. If Jesus would simply poof me back to black upon request. My nerves started to kick in. What if he said no?

As we reached the bleachers, Deanté sat down first and looked up at me like Hampton did when he was a puppy. This was a boy who wanted something.

He took my hand and feather tingles ran up my spine. "I'm glad. Sit. I have something to tell you." I squeezed in close, though there was plenty of room. "I wanted to kiss you that day at the probate. I didn't because . . . well, because I . . ."

"You're not really white, are you?"

He laughed. "No. I should have kissed you last year or the year before that or the year before that. I've wanted to for that long. You're the strangest girl that I know."

"Gee, thanks."

"That's not what I meant. No, strange like the best kind of strange." He lifted his hand to my cheek. "Like . . . special, or wonderful. I'll kiss you tomorrow. When you look like you're supposed to look, taste like you're supposed to taste, smell like you're supposed to smell. Then I'll kiss you."

I eased his hand away from my face and planted a soft but passionate kiss on his lips. My hands floated to his hair, shorter than my shortest fingernail, soft as cotton. My pinkie made its way to the deep-dish dimple on the left side of his cheek, where it ate my entire nail. His lips were full and he tasted like minty toothpaste. This should have been my first kiss. Whether it lasted a minute or an hour I couldn't tell. I knew that this was who I was supposed to be with.

The ocean whooshed and we pulled apart. "I'm sad that's over," I said.

His eyes were still closed. "Me too."

"Open your eyes," I said. "We have to get back."

On the way back, we held hands and laughed about the day ahead. We agreed that Alex was a genius.

The intercom blared. "Toya Williams, please report to the principal's office. Toya Williams, please report to the principal's office."

Deanté said, "Uh-oh, should you go?"

"It's probably about tardiness. I'll just walk by and see if it looks serious. You go on to class." I planted a public kiss on Deanté's lips. "What the hell, right?"

"That's right." He flashed his dimple and I took a mental note to stick my pinkie in there again tomorrow.

When I reached the office, Mom and Dad stood in the lobby, holding on to each other. Mom looked like she would fall over if he wasn't standing sturdy for support. I had never seen him support her, ever. When I got closer, I saw that both of their eyes were bloodshot and puffy. In that moment, curiosity turned to terror.

"What are you doing here?" I dropped my book bag and ran to them.

"I called them." The Gatekeeper had long abandoned her catalog shopping.

"Katarina, have you seen Alex?" asked the principal, standing two feet away in all his glory.

"Who the hell is Katarina?" Mom inquired.

Dad leaned into Mom. "I think that's what she's calling herself now."

Mom stabilized herself, wheeled her arm back, and slapped me so hard that I spun around a full revolution.

"I told you not to abandon your brother!" It was as if every one of her prior screams were practice for that very moment. It was jolting. Her knees buckled and she fell into a heap on the carpet.

"Ma'am, please!" said the principal.

The secretary grabbed his forearm. "No, let them be."

"Forgive her. She's . . ." Dad trailed off, and lifted Mom.

When I oriented myself, the tingle in my cheek disappeared. "What the hell is going on?"

I looked from Mom to Dad. They looked equally disgusted with me.

Dad reached into his pocket and pulled out a folded sheet of paper. I thought it might be one of Alex's letters, but the bright pink markings ruled that out. "This was posted in your brother's ISS cubicle. Among other places. And now we can't find Alex anywhere."

The unmistakable penmanship of Amera and/or Amelia—loopy and bubbly with tiny hearts and stars above the *I*s.

WHO IS ALEX WILLIAMS?

a loser who collects quarters like a child,

steals food from grocery stores, and wears
free shirts with ridiculous sayings on them.

My hands began to tremble. "Where is he?" I asked, still staring at my words.

"Flip it over," Mom said furiously.

I DID IT ALL FOR YOU, TOYA. I'M DONE.
Alex

Dad steadied his voice. "He's gone."

GONE

What a word. *Gone*: two consonants, two vowels; still it packed a profound punch. "What do you mean, 'gone'?" I asked my father.

"We were hoping you had the answer to that question." Dad held on to Mom.

"She didn't even notice he'd left." She gave me the angriest look I'd ever seen from her. "You didn't, did you?"

"When was the last time you spoke to Alex?" asked Dad.

"She's so desperate to hang with these white folks that she probably forgot her brother's name—"

I was going to turn back to black tomorrow and everything was going to be just like it used to be, and Deanté would stop teasing us, and we could just drop out and get GEDs and go to the

George Wallace Community College to get my grades up so we could transfer to wherever in the world we wanted to go to. Alex and Toya. Toya and Alex. We could go to Alabama State and I could pledge Gamma Pi, and he could pledge Gamma Phi. He would like that. He could finally fit. I'd say that we spent more than enough time around white people, so it would be interesting to engulf ourselves in blackness for a bit.

Then again, Alex always had an obsession with big cities, so maybe we could go off to New York University. If I made straight As in junior college and never missed a day or was late ever, maybe they'd let us go together. Or he could go to Harvard and I could find another, less-smart-people college in Boston so that I could be near him. It was a trick. Jesus was just teaching me a quick lesson, and let me tell you something, it *totally* worked. All I wanted in the world was my big brother. I didn't have to breathe or walk or speak or eat or drink or kiss or shower or anything ever again as long as I could have my big brother back.

"Jesus?" When I spoke, I realized I was running. I'd never been much of a runner, but I'd made it to the shadowy part of the woods on the way to our empty castle. Surely Alex was there waiting, in on the joke. "Jesus? Jesus? *Jesus!*"

I never knew one person had so many tears inside them.

Braveheart tears were child's play in comparison. I wept the longest, hardest cry of my life, and I looked forward to the dry headache that followed, knowing that meant it was over.

The strangest vision flew through my head. Bella Swan, from the Twilight series, lying in the woods for four chapters waiting for Edward, the vampire, to return. Those chapters were the boringest in the series, so I got up and walked toward the road.

"Hey," Jesus said.

"Don't give me that crap. Where have you been? I called you!"

"I heard you," he said.

I let a few moments pass before I spoke. "Okay. If you heard me, why didn't you help me?"

"I gave you what you asked."

I couldn't believe that he'd tried to teach a lesson in a time like that. "I get it. I'm a horrible sinner, but would you mind returning my brother, please?" I needed to believe that it was possible; it was holding me together. "Actually, just erase the last few weeks so I can do it all again."

"I cannot do that," he replied simply.

I let out a nervous laugh. "You must be joking. You can turn a black girl whatever race she asks, you can hear millions of prayers at once, and you can't bring my big brother back to me? Tell me where he is!" Involuntary tears streamed down my face. I never hiccuped or shoulder-jerked at all; they simply fell out of my eyes like raindrops from the open sky. "Tell me what to do."

"I can't say."

"So why are you here? Go away! It's all your fault! You ruined everything. You let me turn into this! I was happier before; I had my brother and my mom and dad, and *Unsolved Mysteries* and Alabama Thrift. Leave me alone." My nails dug into the gravel, unloosing tiny rocks mixed with asphalt from the surface. I couldn't even tell how I'd wound up on the ground, but my knees ached, so I assumed I'd fallen hard knee-first. "Actually, before you go, turn me back into Toya!"

Jesus gently placed his hand on my forehead.

The change couldn't have taken more than a minute. I felt my lengthy blond hair being drawn back into my scalp like a pasta maker in reverse. The pigment tingled just below the surface of my skin, pushing through the white. My thighs thickened a bit, making my jeans tug at the seams. And a quick breeze inched my ear, which was no longer covered by a sheet of hair.

I looked up at him. "It's all my fault, isn't it? It is." I crawled toward the woods to lean on a thick tree trunk.

"It's not that simple, Latoya. I just need you to know that you have a lot left to do here. You're supposed to be on this Earth for a while, and I'm here so you don't do anything stupid." The last part shocked me. I would never imagine Jesus using the word *stu-pid* in any situation.

"How am I supposed to live in a place where my brother despises me?" It was a grief that I couldn't explain. A pain worse than pain. I turned toward Jesus. "Why didn't you tell him to talk to me? What kind of God are you?"

"One that you should trust."

He'd stumped me. Maybe because I didn't have any other option or maybe because I couldn't think of anything other than the pain.

"You didn't tell me" was all I could think to say.

"You know that I couldn't," he replied. "You didn't heed my warnings." It may have been cruel timing, but he was right: Him, my mom, even Deanté tried, but I was too preoccupied with myself to pay attention to my ailing brother. Jesus walked toward me and rubbed my upper back. I lifted myself up with the help of the tree.

"Now go home," he said.

I began walking. I didn't think of how long it would take or the fact that I wasn't wearing the appropriate shoes. I just did as Jesus instructed. A few steps along the path, I saw it. A shiny, glowing quarter peeking through the dirt. A single beam of sunlight penetrated the woods, so I held the found quarter to the sun. Its outer grooves were pronounced, like it had never suffered a fall.

Its president smiled a tiny bit wider than on regular quarters, and he looked more platinum than silver. I slid the quarter safely into my pocket, and then I saw another. When I bent down to pick it up, I saw another one, leading deeper into the woods. Three or four feet to the right of that one lay another, and then another, and another. An hour or so later, my hands and pockets were overflowing with brand-new shining quarters.

Hope.

When I finally reached the edge of the woods, Gus Von March stood in the distance, but the quarters led the way to the empty castle. After a few more miles, they became less frequent—one every half block or so. Then, at the base of Colossus, they disappeared altogether, so I went around. I just couldn't find the strength to take it on alone.

I saw Dad's Fiat parked haphazardly in front of the house. Hampton didn't run up the driveway to meet me like he usually did; he staked out the mailbox instead, waiting. I ran to my room. Mom yelled after me until Dad told her to give me space—she actually listened for once. I sat long enough for the sun to sink and the spider to construct the most intricate web I'd ever seen from her. "All the other spider ladies are going to be so jealous."

I heard more than two voices downstairs, but none of them was Alex. They sounded like my evil aunt Evilyn and cousin Joyce, who'd made the trip all the way from Tuscaloosa for some mess.

They'd never understood Alex. They seemed to think he was strange or weird, so their presence pissed me off.

The doorbell rang for the first time in months, which meant someone knew to stick something long and sharp in the hole where the button used to be. Alex! I opened my bedroom door to stand at the top of the stairs, but it wasn't Alex. It was our handyman neighbor, Hank, who had never bothered to come by our broken house since we'd moved in, but there he was when someone went missing.

Everyone stopped their conversations to gawk at me. I just walked back into my room.

When the door almost met the catch, Evilyn said, "That poor gal. How's she doing, Cam?"

I reopened the door. "Ha! You don't care how I'm doing, and you know it! You're just here because your old, decrepit ass doesn't have anything better to do, and my missing brother trumps reruns of *Family Feud*. Well, I think this is just cruel, you showing up after all the hell you've put me and Alex through. Since you're being cruel today, I'll just be honest. Evilyn, freshman year you told me that I looked like a man. Your words changed the course of my life and ruined my self-esteem from that moment on. I looked up to you, you foul old bat. As for the rest of you, why are you even here? You hate Alex. How dare you all stand in my father's home? My father, the same man you called a loser, a failure, an idiot, or worse.

Go home. All of you low-down, sorry, sad excuses for family members. You too, Hank!" I slammed my bedroom door behind me.

My dad kindly escorted every one of them from our home. He never swore or raised his voice, but he started with "You heard her, out." Mom mostly sobbed into the pillows. Meanwhile, I sat on my two-seater, counting my quarters. I counted and recounted all night long. Never slept or lay down or even moved from that one spot. I just sat there upright, counting, until the spider undid her masterpiece and the sun peeked through the trees. Thirteen dollars exactly.

There was a vigorous knock on the door and yelling from the front porch. Dad opened the door. "Yes?" Dad's voice was tired and worn.

"It's Deanté. I'm here for Toya." His voice was frantic.

"You are welcome in my home," said Dad. My heart melted for my father, who had rarely welcomed a soul into his house but allowed my friend over the threshold without question.

He banged on my bedroom door. "Toya!"

"Come in," I replied weakly.

He found me sitting cross-legged, surrounded by my quarters. He stopped at the entrance to my room.

Deanté said, "You look like you again." His eyes were glassy.

"They're his favorite, you know? He hates dimes, he says they're too small and easy to lose. They'd slip right through his fingers when he tried to put them in the drink machine at school. Nickels, Lord knows he's always despised nickels. His nickname for nickels was Jan Brady, or the middle child." I chuckled while Deanté just stood there, looking horrified. "You get it? They're sort of like fillers when a dime is too high and a penny's too low. They're stuck in the middle of all of it. They don't quite fit into the flow of things, kind of like him." I took a breath to make sure that I still could. "Pennies were the worst, because they made his hands smell like butthole, he said. Weird, though, he always said that if he had a daughter, he would name her Penny." I held a quarter in the air. "He revered the quarters. Every so often, he'd spout on about their usefulness: arcade games, air hockey, bubble gum machines, parking meters, McChickens, Quarter Pounders, laundry—he could go on and on like Bubba could about shrimp. The quarters made sense; I thought . . ." My voice cracked from too many hours without water, and I broke, right there on my bedroom floor. "I thought they'd lead me to him."

Deanté lifted me in his arms and placed me gently on my twin bed. He sat with me until I fell asleep.

YOU'RE WEIRD, BUT I LIKE YOU

The next hours were a blur. One of God's ways of protecting us from overwhelming hurt was a short attention span. Ask any mother to describe the pain of childbirth and she can't remember it. I do recall Deanté's vague account of Josh crapping his pants and the twins being kicked out of show choir. Apparently Mr. Holder made a dramatic scene in rehearsal, telling them how they could never be his Dolly P.'s, because Dolly was as sweet as pecan pie and they were bitter Louisiana lemons. Deanté seemed confused by the reference, but I understood perfectly.

Mom and Dad treated me like a Fabergé egg: lovely, irreplaceable, and breakable. Mom kept apologizing for the slap and Dad kept telling her to quit apologizing. Meanwhile, I was mostly worried about them. I'd always thought they were ill-equipped to deal with most of life's curveballs—but they surprised me. Mom spent the remainder of that night screaming and crying, but afterward flooded social media from the bathroom computer. Dad retreated into himself, walking for hours and quietly going about the business of paying for the empty castle. The most reassuring thing about my parents was they watched that night's episode of *Unsolved Mysteries*. In the major ways, they didn't change, which I appreciated more than they knew.

"My God." I shot up from my bed, startling Deanté, who had fallen asleep on the carpet. Had we slept the whole day away?

"What is it?" he asked, alarmed.

"Mrs. Roseland!" I threw the covers from my legs. "Has anyone spoken to Mrs. Roseland?"

"What? I don't think so. Why?"

I ran down the stairs, yelling, "Someone needs to call Mrs. Roseland. She's the Alabama History teacher. Someone find her number and call her right now!"

I walked in on Mom, Dad, and Aunt Evilyn gathered around the kitchen counter, stapling flyers.

"I'm sorry," said Aunt Evilyn. She clutched her purse and held it over her chest. "I'll let y'all alone to talk. I wanted to help."

"Aunt Evilyn?" I asked.

"Yes, little girl?"

"Is Mrs. Roseland still in your bowling league?"

"Betsy?"

"I have no idea what her first name is," I replied. "Wears bright red lipstick and kitten heels?"

"That's Betsy," said Aunt Evilyn. "She's in my league."

"Do you have her telephone number?"

She smiled, obviously eager to help in some way. "I'll check," she said without making eye contact.

As she thumbed through her wallet-sized address book, Dad asked, "Why Mrs. Roseland?"

"I overheard them talking. She's his Jesus." I began pacing the kitchen. "She may have helped him."

"Your cheek has my handprint on it," Mom interjected. "I'm so sorry."

"Mom. Later. Please."

"I found it," announced Aunt Evilyn.

"Deanté, give me your phone," I said.

I dialed the numbers as Aunt Evilyn called them out. The telephone rang and rang, but there was no answer. "Do you have the address, too?"

Aunt Evilyn nodded. "I've dropped her off at home a time or two. She's just a few streets over. Only pink house on Kensington."

"Deanté?"

He grabbed his car keys. "Let's go." We ran to his mother's Mercedes, while my mother and Aunt Evilyn squeezed into the Fiat with Dad.

The sun was setting as we pulled up to the only baby-pink house on Kensington Boulevard, Mrs. Roseland's car parked in the driveway. When we rolled to a stop, I immediately jumped out, leaving Deanté in the car.

"Should we wait on your parents? They were behind me, but I think something may have gone wrong with the car."

I was already halfway up the sidewalk, approaching the pale-green front door. "Go check on them. I'll be here."

I pressed the bronzed doorbell. "Coming, coming, coming," I heard Mrs. Roseland chirp from inside.

Mrs. Roseland peeked through the right-most curtain and quickly cracked the door. "Toya, Toya, Toya! I'm happy to see you're back."

"Is Alex here, Mrs. Roseland?" I blurted. "He's missing."

"He's in the in-law suite out back. He was waiting here when I got home from school on Tuesday. I heard him call your mom and tell her." She saw my shock, and she held her palm to her lips. "He tricked me."

I stormed off the wraparound porch and pushed the fence open. "Alex!" I howled.

In the distance, the Fiat sputtered to the curb, followed by Deanté's Mercedes. Alex opened the suite door and wiped the sleep from his eyes. He wore green plaid pajama pants and a faded T-shirt that read *Hello Courage*. "How did you find me?" He gawked at me, squinting.

"The principal found your note in your cubicle."

"Dang."

"Dang is right," I said. "He gave it to Mom and Dad, and Mom made a scene at school. The Gatekeeper put down her magazine to watch." I smiled.

"So that's what it takes for her to put down that catalog?"

"That's nothing. Mom slapped me!"

"Shoot! I hate that I missed it."

I laughed. "I'm sure you do." I reached into my pocket, pulled out a quarter I'd found in the woods, and held it to him.

He placed it back in my palm and closed my hand around it. "How many did you find?" he asked, staring at the ground. "I left most of them in the woods."

"Thirteen dollars' worth."

"There's more." He smiled faintly.

"Alex! You're all right!" Mom nearly knocked me down to get to her son. "Let me look at you," she said, inspecting his arms, legs, and face.

"I'm fine, Mom."

"You scared us, kid." Dad stood a few feet away, unable to move any closer.

Even when I'd humiliated and abandoned him, he still thought to leave me his shiniest quarters. I felt undeserving of such a sibling. I took a few steps away from them to stand near the fence with Aunt Evilyn, who was still clutching her purse.

"You've grown up to be kind of pretty," she told me. "You weren't too pretty when you were little, but I shouldn't have told you to your face."

It was the best Aunt Evilyn had to offer. I'd take it.

FIERCE

Later that night, I checked on my spider. After hours of spinning and weaving geometric shapes, she perched herself in the center to reap the benefits of her magnificent work. She truly was fierce.

I opened my spider's window a half an inch. "Hey there. I've been watching you for a while, and I just wanted to let you know that I think you're freaking awesome. I love what you do with your web; it's gorgeous, and you will always have a place on my window as long as you would like. But never—and I repeat, never—come into my room or I'll squash you without a second thought." I carefully closed the window and latched it shut.

Afterward, I powered up the computer in the bathroom. The Wi-Fi was running faster than I'd ever seen it. It only took fifteen minutes to log in to my hardly used e-mail account, then another twelve to look up the e-mail address to north-central Alabama's NPR news station, based in Birmingham. That station housed the Southern Education Desk, which said it was *committed to exploring the challenges and opportunities confronting education in the twenty-first century.*

I gulped down one deep breath and caught my reflection behind the bulky computer. I focused on my large dark eyes, almost black but not quite. I hadn't realized it, but my eyes were beautiful. No. Fierce!

> To: Sam Watson
> From: Toya Williams
> SUBJECT: Do with this information what you will
> Dear Mr. Watson at the Southern Education Desk,
> I am a student at Edgewood High School in
> Montgomery, AL. I recently reported an attempted
> rape to my principal, Principal Smith at Edgewood
> High School, and nothing was done about it.
> Since the boy, Joshua Anderson, belongs to a well-
> respected Edgewood family, the principal rejected
> my claim. Joshua is the son of the owner of Anderson
> Toyota, Jeep, Dodge.
> I'm writing you because though I was saved from
> outright rape, I fear this boy has and will continue to

pursue other victims. I fear that I am forever changed
by this incident, but I would feel accountable if I
didn't take further action in this matter, and God
forbid, another girl is victimized.

I am contacting you first, but if you do not respond to
this e-mail within a week, I will pass the story along to
another station. If they don't respond, I will pursue
media outside the state. In other words, Mr. Watson,
I will not stop until Joshua Anderson and Principal
Smith are exposed. I would appreciate your help, but
if you are not receptive, I'll find someone who is.

Thank you for your time.

Sincerely,

T.M.W.

My finger hovered over the send button, and I considered
erasing the e-mail, shutting down the computer, and walking away,
but then swallowed. The lump in my throat had shrunk from pea-
sized to the size of a small seed. But it was still there.

Message sent.

I peeked in on Alex. He appeared to be fast asleep.

"You up?"

"I'm up." He pulled his covers up around his chin.

I stepped inside and stood in the center of the bedroom. "I know you're going off to the big city."

He sat up in his bed, still grasping his comforter.

"Before you go, I just want to let you know that you're the most important person in my life. I'm not a good sister. I realize that. But somehow, as horrible as I am, I was blessed with the most wonderful brother in the wide world. I'm so proud of you." I clenched my hands into tight fists, fighting the urge to yelp. "I love you, Alexander Williams."

I ran downstairs and screamed for my mother and father.

They burst from their room, terrified. "It's three in the morning. What's going on?" Dad said.

"Oh my God! What's wrong, Toya? Is it Alex?" Mom panicked.

"Are you guys sleeping in the same bedroom?" They looked at each other and shrugged.

"Mom, you're loud and strange and mean to Dad when he doesn't deserve it, but I love you more than you will ever understand. You're the most beautiful woman I've ever seen and the most wonderful mother I could ever ask for. I know that you had a moment of doubt—everyone does. Get over it, I love you no matter what you do, and so does Dad." Mom glanced over at Dad and smiled.

Then I turned to Dad. "No one understands you. You never

pick up on social cues, and you do disgusting things like spill coffee on your floor and pee all over the toilet seat."

Mom interrupted, "Who you tellin'?"

"Mom! Anyways, as I was saying. Yes, you have flaws, but you also love us enough to work double overtime so we can live in a good neighborhood and go to the best school in Alabama, even though it's a terrible place. You have trouble showing it, but I want you to know that I know, you know? I know you love me so much it hurts, and I feel the same way." I gave them both high fives, because I knew hugs would be too overwhelming for them. "Now, there's something that I have to do."

"What?" Mom said, fighting back emotion. Dad stood there with his mouth open.

"I have to go conquer Colossus." I turned and walked out the front door.

"You don't have any shoes on. What are you—?"

"Mom! I have to do this. Give me twenty minutes. If I'm not back by then, come get me."

"Let her go, Mom," Alex announced from the top of the stairs.

She took a step back. "Okay."

"All right. And I'm taking Hampton."

Hampton was waiting on the doorstep. I swear that dog had more sense than anyone gave him credit for. I knelt down to him. "I'm sorry that I've been such a horrible friend to you. Alex is the love of your life, I know that, and I'm a crappy replacement, but he's leaving for a while. I promise to do my best by you." I held the leash open for him to walk through. "Will you have me?" He tilted his head and walked through the collar to accept. "Good deal, let's go."

I walked the length of my street at three thirty in the morning. A gentle breeze made the leaves dance, and the Montgomery heat pulled beads of sweat from my forehead. Hampton didn't tug his leash at all; he walked at my heels as if knowing the magnitude of the moment. I stood at the top of Colossus peering over, and I knew. We had to run it.

I dropped Hampton's leash and knelt to him. "Look, I'll take your leash off. I think we should both be free when we do this. I'm not going to lie to you, this is going to suck." I unhooked the leash and tossed it in the grass.

"Ready? Set. Go!"

Jogging down the hill was not easy. I pointed my feet to keep from falling, and when I caught my stride, I focused on the stiff wind blowing in my face. I opened my arms to hug the air. The wind caught Hampton's jowls and turned his mouth into an enormous smile. We reached the bottom in no time, which meant it was time to truly conquer Colossus.

I turned my head to the sky and said, "Thank you, Jesus."

Then we took off. The first few strides made me want to give up. Every muscle in my legs, arms, butt, and stomach was working at capacity to keep me upright and running, but my mind was fixed on my big brother: his potential, his retention, his brilliance. I had always envisioned Alex as a sweater-vest-wearing history teacher at the community college, sharing his braininess with eager teenagers, but even then, I hadn't given him enough credit.

I assumed he wanted to be popular, but he was reaching for something that I didn't know existed—a world outside of Edgewood. He was shaping his life into something that would break the barriers of humanity, not just of the South. While I was asking God to change me, he was utilizing what he was born with to conquer all things. The least I could do was conquer Colossus. We made up the chant after we finally walked it without stopping, and there I was, running it. Alone.

If I cried, I wouldn't finish, so I fought hard to stop the tears from coming.

"YOU STOP IT! Cry when you get to the top!" I screamed in one long, impossible breath. I was three-fourths of the way up. Pushing through the physical pain was easy; stopping the emotion was excruciating.

Alex tried so hard to make me smart. I'd always thought he was bragging about his own God-given genius, but I realized he just wanted me to go on the journey with him. He was trying to lift me up. Help me accept myself.

Hampton reached the top a few seconds before I did. He tried to collapse. "No! Not until we chant."

He stood tall. *"Woof!"*

"Good boy," I said, tears burning at the corners of my eyes.

I stood there for a moment, thinking of myself two weeks ago and just how badly I'd wanted to be something else. Anyone other than Toya. How I'd asked my mother to change my name and asked God to turn me into something better. How foolish I was to ignore the one person who accepted me for exactly who I was, no matter what. I studied my sweat-drenched body and bare feet. My jagged toenails and half-bitten fingernails. My unshaven arms and legs. Closed my eyes and ran my fingers through the short hair that I'd loathed for so long. Opened my eyes to my skin. The color of a brown Crayola crayon or coffee with a single hit of cream.

I looked toward Hampton. "I have to change our chant."

"Woof!"

I assumed the position. Two fists in the air, legs spread apart, and *Rocky* feet planted firmly on the ground.

> *"Colossus, the Great.*
> *I am strong.*
> *I am able.*
> *I am God's child.*
> *I am who I am.*

I am who I say I am.

I am black.

I am beautiful.

I am me.

I am . . .

Toya."

ACKNOWLEDGMENTS

I've always been an odd girl with an odd perspective. I see the world differently from everyone else, and since that can be isolating, I learned to bury my strangeness. Pageant-waving my way through life and nodding along to viewpoints I didn't agree with or understand. Shrinking myself to the back of the room and allowing the louder voices to dominate. I accept that I'll never be the loudest voice, but I have a secret weapon (well, it's not so secret anymore): I write.

So my first, and most important, thank-you is reserved for my strangeness. I've buried you, covered you up, put lipstick on your face and high heels on your ailing feet. Still, you've never left me alone. I couldn't have written a word of this book without you. I couldn't have married the most beautiful human being in the world without you. I would be as boring as Barnhouse's biology without you. And I want you to know, once and for all, I'm done hiding behind your twin sister, normal. I vow to hold you in my arms for the rest of my life.

A special thanks to my editor, Liz Szabla. Your patience, kindness, and incredible insight have transformed this book. You're a brilliant woman, and I appreciate you more than you can ever know. Thank you to my publisher, Jean Feiwel, for welcoming me to Feiwel and Friends with such warmth! To the spectacular team at the Macmillan Children's Publishing Group: You amaze me every day. Thank you for working tirelessly to bring so many stunning books into the world.

To Marietta Zacker, agent extraordinaire: Thank you for helping me move forward when everything inside of me wanted to quit. For your encouragement, wise counsel, and overall awesomeness, I thank you.

To Kerry Madden and the Spring 2013 Children's Literature Workshop: You made me believe, Kerry. Through your passionate instruction, you've made us all believe. We made magic happen every week in that class, and I'm looking forward to following all your bright and beautiful writing careers.

To the Night Writers: Thank you all so much for awesome insights and unyielding support. There's something really special happening in our group! And I'm so proud of us. Special thanks